"It's not as though this is some kind of love match."

She winced as she said that, as though what she had felt for him and still felt could be dismissed in a few well-chosen words. "However strong your sense of duty is, I don't intend to fall victim to it."

"This isn't about *you,* though, is it?" He turned to face her then. "And it isn't about whether I wanted to become a daddy or not. The reality is that you're pregnant with my baby and I intend to take care of the situation."

"This is not a *situation,*" Mattie told him, but a small, treacherous side of her longed to be taken care of. It was the same small, treacherous side that had told her she could handle a man like Dominic. Wisdom would be to avoid that small, treacherous side like the plague.

"Event. Occurrence. Happening. Call it whatever you want to, but whatever you decide to call it, you're not running away from me this time."

GREEK TYCOONS

**They're the men who have everything—
except a bride...**

Wealth, power, charm—
what else could a heart-stoppingly handsome
tycoon need? In THE GREEK TYCOONS miniseries
you have already met some gorgeous Greek
multimillionaires who are in need of wives.

Now it's the turn of talented Presents author
Cathy Williams, with her feisty
and passionate romance
The Greek Tycoon's Secret Child

This tycoon has met his match, and he's decided
he *has* to have her...*whatever* that takes!

Coming soon in Harlequin Presents:

The Greek's Virgin Bride
by Julia James
March #2383

The Mistress Purchase
by Penny Jordan
April #2386

The Stephanides Pregnancy
by Lynne Graham
May #2392

Cathy Williams

THE GREEK TYCOON'S SECRET CHILD

GREEK
TYCOONS

HARLEQUIN®

TORONTO • NEW YORK • LONDON
AMSTERDAM • PARIS • SYDNEY • HAMBURG
STOCKHOLM • ATHENS • TOKYO • MILAN • MADRID
PRAGUE • WARSAW • BUDAPEST • AUCKLAND

ISBN 0-373-12376-0

THE GREEK TYCOON'S SECRET CHILD

First North American Publication 2004.

CHAPTER ONE

DOMINIC DRECOS hadn't expected to like this sort of place. In fact, he had always been contemptuous of those high-flying businessmen who played at happy families while taking time out to frequent the sort of nightclub that offered them the opportunity to ogle beautiful young women, dressed in next to nothing, for the price of some very expensive alcohol. The sort of place where a woman sold her dignity for ridiculous tips. In fact, a nightclub pretty much like this.

But he hadn't been able to get out of this. His very important client, along with his entourage of two accountants and three board directors, had insisted.

They wanted to see London at night, by which they had not been referring to a refined restaurant in Knightsbridge followed by a stroll through Piccadilly Circus. Nor had they meant an evening of culture at one of the theatres in Drury Lane.

'Where the hell am I supposed to take them?' he had asked his secretary in frustration. 'Do I look like the sort of man who goes to places like that? And before you answer that one, remember that your job may be on the line.' But he had grinned at his fifty-five-year-old secretary. 'I don't suppose you could recommend somewhere? Do you go to places like that?'

'Don't think they allow grannies in, Mr Drecos,' Gloria had said with commendable seriousness. 'I'll ask around and find somewhere appropriate.'

It had been to her credit that she had managed to find

one that, at least, had not involved any erotic table dancing or live performances in overhead cages. Thank heavens.

In fact, he thought now as he looked around him with the obligatory glass of champagne in his hand, aside from the minuscule dress code of the waitresses, the place wasn't too sordid. The lighting was a little subdued, admittedly, but the food had been passable enough and if the drinks were outrageously priced, then what the hell?

This particular deal was worth a substantial amount of money, and his client appeared to be having a good enough time.

And it had to be said that the array of gorgeous waitresses paraded before him were manna to his jaded soul.

Dominic Drecos had had it when it came to meaningful involvement with members of the opposite sex. Just the thought of his ex-girlfriend was still enough to bring him out in a cold sweat, even though he had, thank heavens, neither seen nor heard anything of her for the past six months.

No, sir. Conversation. Intimate meals out. Theatres, presents and the whole paraphernalia of courtship could take a running leap as far as he was concerned.

He forced himself back into conversation with his client, asked politely interested questions about his Oxford University education, and glanced discreetly at his watch.

It was when he looked up that he saw her.

She was standing by their table, tray balanced, naturally, on her hip, body inclined slightly forward. Typical ploy of the waitresses, he had drily observed earlier on. They leaned over to take orders, revealing a tantalising amount of cleavage, in many cases cleavage that seemed to owe their existence to science rather than nature, smiling provocatively as they encouraged the punters to fling their money away on champagne. They would, of course, be taking a cut of each bottle they managed to entice out of their customers.

This one was using the same tired ploy, along with the same smile, same tilt of the head, but he hadn't noticed her before.

Where had she come from? She certainly hadn't been in evidence at their table before now. No, that girl had been a brunette of ample proportions and wickedly provocative eyes.

'Can I interest you gentlemen in some of our champagne?' she coaxed now, in a voice like slowly burning smoke.

Dominic was amused and slightly surprised to find that the question running through his head was what else she had on offer of interest. To him.

Surprised because since Rosalind he had managed to conduct a very celibate existence, untempted by the many women with whom he came into contact on virtually a daily basis. Either through his very hectic social life or through the myriad business dos that he was obliged to attend.

Her eyes flitted around the group of men and found Dominic's and, as if reading the message lazily conveyed in his broodingly dark gaze, she looked away quickly and straightened ever so slightly.

'Perhaps a couple more bottles?' His client sat back in his chair, knowing that his question was more in the nature of a flat statement. None of his henchmen would dare query the need for yet more champagne and Dominic, who would easily have made known his thoughts on any such thing, found himself readily agreeing.

'Why not?' He was finding it difficult to tear his eyes away from the blonde.

She wasn't just good-looking. Good-looking blondes were a dime a dozen. She was exotically unusual. Slimmer than most of the other waitresses in the place, with a lean, boyish frame that should have lent her an androgynous look but didn't because her face was just too damn feminine. Heart-shaped, with a short, straight nose, very large, almond-shaped eyes whose colour he couldn't discern because of the discreet lighting, and framed by the most amazing hair he had ever seen. Hair the colour of vanilla, poker-straight and almost waist-length.

He relaxed back in the chair, all the better to survey her, aware that he was now behaving like one of those sad old businessmen he had mentally sneered at earlier on.

She was, he noticed, making sure not to look in his direction. Which he found just a bit irritating, partly because he was footing the bill for the very expensive and highly unnecessary champagne she had succeeded in persuading them to buy and partly because he was accustomed to being looked at by women.

So he said now, in a smooth drawl, 'But that's the last of the champagne, my darling. Some of us have a full day's work in the morning.' An equally smooth half-smile accompanied that remark.

He heard the patronising arrogance in his voice and winced, but hell, anything to get her to look at him.

Celibacy, he thought with wry amusement, must really be kicking in if he now found himself reduced to trying to commandeer the attention of a waitress in a nightclub.

But it worked. She looked at him and he could see the need to appear friendly warring with cold distaste. She began gathering the empty glasses onto her tray, and as she turned for his she leaned slightly forward, offering him a glimpse of generous cleavage that looked all natural, and said in a sibilant, deadly whisper,

'I'm not *your darling.*' Then she was standing up again, the bland smile back on her face, and heading off into the shadows.

How dared he? Mattie thought furiously. Of course, she had encountered that sort of thing before. Well-oiled businessmen with eyes on stalks, thinking that they could talk to her in whatever suggestive voice they wanted.

For the most part, she had learnt to ignore them. She was a waitress, whatever her outfit of high shoes and small, tight dress might indicate to the contrary, and there was a strict policy of not fraternising with the customers.

But their customers didn't usually come wrapped up like that one. Something about him had made the hairs on the back of her neck stand on end, and the lazy contempt she had heard in his voice had fired up a part of her that should have known better. After all, she had been working in the place for nearly seven months now, way long enough to know how to handle seedy customers.

Not that he had looked seedy. Too good-looking for that. But she of all people ought to know that good looks could cover a multitude of sins.

She found that she was glowering at Mike as he replaced two empty bottles of champagne for another two.

'What's up, gorgeous?' he asked, grinning, and Mattie smiled back a weak smile.

'Oh, the usual.'

'Ah.' A nod of understanding. 'Just ignore him.' He began handing her clean flutes. 'Filthy minds. Probably has some poor wife waiting up for him at home and a handful of kiddies.'

'Look, can Jessie handle that table? I really can't deal with that sort right now.' One particularly bad row with Frankie, a course project with a deadline she was finding it difficult to meet, did not add up for a whole lot of patience when it came to difficult customers.

'No chance.' Mike looked at her ruefully. 'The place is heaving and we're two girls short. Which is why you're working that table in the first place, with Jackie leaving like that. Old Harry's fit to explode as it is. If you value your life, I'd just put up with the bastard. He'll clear off soon enough.'

Easier said than done. She weaved her way back over to the table, her jaw aching from the effort of trying to appear natural. Harry did not approve of his girls looking anything but bright-eyed and bushy-tailed. As if they were enjoying every minute of having to serve drinks to inebriated, rich men whilst dressed in outfits that invited lurid comments and lecherous remarks.

Sometimes it all just seemed too much.

But the money was brilliant. That was one thing she couldn't afford to forget.

And she needed the money.

And how many other night jobs could offer what she got at this place? Because a day job was out of the question. Too much of her time during the day was used up with completing her course, and what part of the day was left was devoted to sleeping.

Not that she had been getting much of that recently.

She thought of Frankie, knowing that something

would have to be done very soon about him, but, as always, the minute she started thinking of him her brain began to rear up at the logical course of her thought processes, and closed down.

The man appeared to be involved in an intense conversation with his friends when she arrived at his table, which was a blessing, and she was given only a fleeting glance as she expertly opened the champagne and filled their glasses.

But he continued to jar on her mind. She found her eyes straying over to him as she waited on her other tables, watching the way he leaned into his conversation, commanding attention. Still managing to command it even when he drew back, drumming restlessly on the table with one hand whilst the other caressed the champagne flute.

People were beginning to filter out now. It wouldn't be long before she could make her escape. It was a financial disadvantage to leave before the bitter end, as she was inevitably doing herself out of much needed tips from those groups who turned up in the early hours of the morning, but she needed the sleep. Needed the time to restore some energy back into her body. She was young, but she wasn't made of iron and, unlike the other girls working the tables, she didn't have hours of unimpeded sleep ahead of her in which to recover.

She watched covertly as they finished the champagne, hoped that there would not be another bottle ordered even if she was doing herself out of money in the process, walked over towards them, taking a deep breath on the way.

Training was given to all the girls when they first joined on walking. She had never, in her twenty-three years of life, known that there were different ways of

walking. She had always narrowed it down to simply
putting one foot in front of the other. But she had picked
up the style quickly enough so that now, as she headed
towards their table, her gait was unconsciously provocative, all the more so because of her slenderness.

Dominic followed her progress with leisurely enjoyment. She was determined not to look at him. He could
see it in the way she collected their glasses. Nor was she
interested in them ordering another bottle of champagne,
even though she asked the question in the same breathlessly tempting voice.

'Now, where,' he drawled, capturing her reluctant attention, 'do you suggest I put this?' He rested one elbow
on the table and heard his client chuckle with wicked
amusement as he watched the notes between Dominic's
long fingers.

Mattie stretched out her palm.

'Isn't it customary to slip it somewhere rather more
intimate?'

'No.' Mattie flashed him a smile of pure ice and
prayed that Harry wasn't anywhere within earshot.

'Fair enough.' He surrendered and handed her his extremely generous tip.

Mattie hadn't expected it. He was, after all, a typical
obnoxious customer who felt he had no need to treat
her, a lowly waitress in a nightclub, with anything re-
sembling respect. He shouldn't be capable of smiling at
her with such genuine rueful amusement. As if he could
read her mind and could also see for himself what sort
of picture he had portrayed and how it had conveyed
itself to her.

She felt a second of passing disorientation, then her
fingers curled around the money, well earned as far as
she was concerned, and she was walking away. Out to

the changing room, where she could get rid of her ridiculous outfit, step out of the high shoes which still
pinched her toes even though she should have broken
them in a long time ago, into sensible jeans and the flat
trainers she was so much more comfortable wearing.

'Harry,' she said, when she had changed. He was cir-
cling the room, frowning, making sure that everyone was
happy. 'I'm off now.' Mattie liked Harry. If she hadn't,
she would never have stuck the job out for as long as
she had, but underneath his veneer of ill-tempered boss-
iness, he liked the girls who worked for him and treated
them with fondness and respect.

'You're letting me down, Mattie,' he growled. 'Three
girls short. What's the matter with Jackie, anyway? You
took over from her. She tell you anything? Suddenly
flouncing out like that, leaving me in the lurch.'

'She felt ill. Tired, I expect.' Pregnant, Mattie thought,
wondering how Harry would take the news. Finishing
work at five-thirty in the morning, Mattie was also feeling the strain of her job.

'Why don't you stay on, Mats? Earn yourself a few
extra quid?'

'What, and get even less sleep than I manage to now?'

'You should dump that course of yours,' he grumbled.
'Marketing. Pah! Still, when you get your diploma, or
whatever it is that college is dangling in front of you,
you just make sure you come right back here. Help manage this little joint of mine. Anyway, you'd better go.
No good the punters seeing that their glamorous hostess
wears jeans and trainers.'

Mattie laughed. 'No. It wouldn't do for them to think
that I don't live in tight dresses and high heels,
would it?'

She edged her way out of the crowds, towards the exit.

Dominic, standing to one side by the cloakroom, jacket on, accepting the profuse thanks of his little group of guests for showing them an enjoyable time, almost didn't recognise the slender blonde slipping out of the door, her jacket wrapped firmly around her.

Nor would he, under normal circumstances, have allowed his urge to follow her, catch her up, talk to her, to get the better of him. But being in that nightclub had made him realise something, made him see that the world was full of women, uncomplicated women who might entertain the idea of a brief relationship, no strings attached. Beautiful, uncomplicated women, because what other type of woman worked in a place like that? Certainly not those of the high-flying society category, such as his ex-girlfriend, who had thoroughly succeeded in purging him of any inclination to have a serious relationship.

Or so he told himself as he impatiently said his goodbyes to his client, one eye on the figure hurrying up the dark street, about to spin round a corner.

It took a bit of swift moving, swift enough to leave him insufficient time to ask himself what precisely he was doing, and then the gap was closing between them. He caught up with her just as she was about to cross the road, then he reached out and stilled her by placing his hand on her arm.

Mattie swung around instantly. It was after midnight and, although the streets were still busy, so were all the muggers. This was their time of night, when people were scurrying to catch cabs and buses, very likely with wallets poking out like beacons from jacket pockets and a bit too much drink in their blood for them to do much about a running assault.

'You!' Her eyes widened, then narrowed in angry suspicion.

An understandable reaction, Dominic thought belatedly, releasing her and drawing back.

'What the hell are you doing? Following me?' She had only seen him sitting down. Now she realised just how tall he was. Well over six feet. Much taller than she was, and she was no shortie at five feet eight. He was also a lot more powerful close up. Under the well-cut jacket, she could sense a finely honed, muscular body.

'If I told Harry about this, he would have your head for breakfast!' She didn't think that anyone, including any of Harry's very efficient bouncers, could have this man's head for breakfast, and he obviously was of the same opinion, because he shot her a look of frank disbelief.

'I accept tips from the punters, *mister,* but that is *all* you're entitled to!' She whipped back around to discover that he was still following her. Although following would have been the wrong word. More like accommodating his long stride to match hers, to keep up perfectly at her level, until they had both crossed the road, at which point she turned to him again, eyes blazing, letting him know in no uncertain terms that he could take his arrogant and more than likely drunken self up some different road, any road that was not the one she happened to be on!

'I've seen your type before, let me tell you, and you disgust me!'

'My type?' Dominic was finding, to his own bemusement, that his instinctive ability to control conversations was being very thoroughly flattened by the spitting

blonde in front of him. She had her hands stuck angrily
in the pockets of her jacket, only removing one to shove
some of that fabulous fair hair away from her face.

He had pursued her because something about her had
turned him on. A lot. And he had wanted to apologise
for the uncultured oaf he had been inside the nightclub,
looking at her with a suggestiveness he knew she had
recognised and been repulsed by. Quite rightly.

However, her attack on him was taking its toll on his
temper, never that long at the best of times.

'My type?' he repeated, in a voice that had sent many
a high-powered business rival ducking for cover. On her,
however, it appeared to have less than zero effect.

'Yes, your type!' Surprisingly, Mattie found that she
was enjoying this. Actually enjoying this! The initial
shock of seeing him, the passing fear that he had followed her for a purpose, had somehow retreated.
Obnoxious, patronising, arrogant boor he might very
well be, but somehow she knew that he was not going
to shove her down a dark alley so that he could have his
wicked way with her.

She felt absolutely free to yell her lungs out at him
and it was feeling very good to do just that. She hadn't
yelled like this in a very long time and she should have.
Instead of just accepting what had been going on in her
personal life, instead of just submitting to the worse kind
of emotional abuse at the hands of Frankie King, she
should have released her pent-up rage and misery in a
good old screaming match. It helped that she was doing
it now. Wrong person but right sentiment.

'Sad losers with too much money who get a kick out
of looking at pretty young girls. Oh, yes, I know your
type. We *all* know your type! You don't want to do
anything, you just want to look, give yourselves a little

fantasy to take back to your miserable homes with your miserable wives and your unfortunate children!'

'What?' Dominic was fast discovering that he hadn't been quite so prepared for a tongue like a whip. She glared ferociously at him, every inch of her bewitching face pouring scorn, and he began to laugh, a real, genuine belly laugh that only made her face tighten in further rage.

She turned on her heel, began to walk away, knowing that he would catch up with her, expecting it.

'You don't take the underground back to your house at this hour, do you?' he asked as he saw where she was heading.

'Go away, you pervert.'

That, for him, was not acceptable. He moved ahead of her and then swung around so that he was barring her path, and he watched as she debated whether she should try and shoot past him, then obviously decide that she wouldn't be able to make it.

'Oh, no, you don't,' he said coldly.

'You're in my way, and if you don't clear off I'm going to scream so loudly that I'll have every policeman within a ten-mile radius racing over to see what's going on!'

'Is that another threat along the lines of telling your Harry, whoever he might be, that I've followed you so that he can send one of his hit men to teach me a lesson?'

'Get out of my way.' She found that she could barely breathe properly with him standing there like that, towering over her, his hard, good-looking face a study in angles and shadows.

'I don't take very kindly to being labelled a pervert.'

'Do I look as though I care what you do or don't take

kindly to?' But she uneasily felt a stab of guilt at the insult she had flung at him. Then she reminded herself that he was nothing but a good-looking face with a squalid mind, or why else would he have followed her out of the nightclub and cornered her on her way to the underground?

'So you label all the men you see in your line of work as perverts, do you?'

'I want to get home. It's late and I don't need to spend time having this conversation with you. Now, excuse me.'

'Why don't you take a taxi to your house?'

'Because, not that it's any of your business, I can't afford the luxury. If I could afford to catch cabs here, there and everywhere, then I wouldn't be working at a nightclub, would I?'

'We're not talking *here, there and everywhere*. We're talking at this hour in central London. The underground isn't a very safe place to be.' Or so he imagined. He, personally, seldom travelled on the underground. He had a driver so that he could work in the back of the car, and when he didn't want to use George he drove himself.

'You would know, would you?' Mattie snapped, reading his mind with staggering accuracy. 'When was the last time you went anywhere on the tube?' She gave a little grunt of pure scorn, at which point his mind told him to just leave the woman alone, to get a grip on himself.

'I was on my way to the underground myself, as it happens,' he heard himself saying, beyond all common sense.

'You're lying.'

'So now I'm a liar and a pervert, am I?'

Mattie glared at him for a further few seconds and

then dodged around him and began striding towards the illuminated underground entrance.

Dominic fell in line.

What the hell was he doing? he asked himself. What did it matter what a waitress in a nightclub thought of him? So what if she was exciting to look at? At the grand old age of thirty-four he should be over all that by now.

But still he found that he was walking alongside her, feeling her impotent anger simmering from every pore of her body, surreptitiously watching the proud tilt of her head, hands still resolutely thrust into her pockets, her bag, which was no more than a weathered knapsack, casually slung over one shoulder.

'Well, goodbye.' Mattie turned to face him as soon as they were in the station, virtually a ghost town at this time in the morning.

It was the first time she was seeing him in light and what she had taken for a good-looking face, not dissimilar to the one that was probably lying, mouth open, empty whisky bottle at the side, waiting for her on the tired sofa in the sitting room, she now realised far exceeded that.

This man, whose name he had not even bothered to tell her because he was, of course, far too high and mighty for such niceties, especially when it came to the fact that he was just out for a good time with a woman he imagined would be an easy lay, went beyond good-looking. He was very firmly placed in the higher regions of staggering.

Faintly olive-skinned, short black hair, eyes that were as dark as midnight and a bone-structure that seemed to have been chiselled lovingly with perfection in mind.

'What stop are you getting off at?'

'Not the same as yours,' Mattie answered smoothly,

turning away and slotting her coins into the ticket machine. She always made sure that her change was ready for when she got to the ticket machine. No fumbling in bags. Not very safe.

'How would you know that?'

'Because I have eyes in my head.' To prove her point, she insolently raked her eyes over his immaculately tailored suit, his handmade shoes, the gold watch on his wrist.

'I'm delivering you to your door,' Dominic said flatly. There was something about this girl that made him concerned for her safety—her insurgency, perhaps. 'So we do happen to be travelling to the same stop after all. And you needn't fear that I shall try and take advantage of you on the way.'

'I don't need an escort.'

Green eyes. The purest green he had ever seen. The suggestive lighting in the nightclub had only given him a glimpse of her. Here, her face crystallised into huge, almond-shaped eyes, a nose sprinkled with freckles and a full mouth that was currently down-turned in an expression of fierce disdain.

'This place is deserted. Or maybe not. Maybe there'll be a few junkies and drunks waiting to get into the same carriage as you. Am I right?'

'I'm touched that you care so much about my welfare, but I do happen to do this particular route four nights a week. I think it's fair to say that I can take care of myself.' She gave him another scornful once-over. 'Probably more than you can take care of *yourself*.'

'More typecasting?'

'Look, it's late,' Mattie said carefully, meeting his eyes and holding them with difficulty. 'I didn't appreciate the way you were looking at me in the nightclub and I don't appreciate the way you followed me out. Can I make myself any clearer? I need to grab some sleep if I'm not to pass out tomorrow.'

'Don't you have all day to catch up on your sleep?' The dark eyes narrowed speculatively on her face and Mattie felt herself blushing. Blushing like a teenager when in fact she was twenty-three years old and had had enough sobering experiences in her life for a cynical outer shell to be well and truly in place.

'I happen to have things to do,' she muttered. 'The world doesn't cater for people who sleep by day and work by night, in case it's missed you. Now, go away.'

'Fine. But I'll be waiting for you tomorrow at the club.'

'Why?'

This was something that was genuinely puzzling her. She had become experienced in a very short space of time in reading the men who patronised the nightclub. They were usually middle-aged, married but not so married that they didn't still lick their lips at the sight of a pretty girl in next to nothing. Harmless men. Then there were the groups of young, rich yuppies. She personally found them a lot more threatening because there was no wife at home waiting, no kiddies tugging on their consciences.

The man standing in front of her didn't seem to fall into either category.

In fact, he struck her as the sort who didn't need to trail behind waitresses in nightclubs or anywhere else for that matter because whatever woman he wanted would come to him with a click of his fingers.

'Because I don't particularly like being categorised without an explanation.' Which beggared the question of why he should give a damn in the first place, but he could tell that that train of thought hadn't occurred to her from the small frown.

'Look at it this way,' he pointed out smoothly, jumping into whatever she had been thinking so that she once more raised her eyes to his. 'How would you feel if I insulted you by implying that since you were a waitress in a nightclub, willing to dress in next to nothing because the less the clothes, presumably the bigger the tips, you were therefore—'

'A cheap tart?' Mattie snapped, interrupting him before he could voice what he had obviously been thinking. 'A woman of easy virtue? Or maybe a woman of *no* virtue altogether? A sad loser who has nothing better to do with her life than whistle it down the drain working for tips in a nightclub?' Yes, they all thought that. All the men who ogled her as she waited their tables. It still got her back up, though.

Not just with him, but with herself because *she* knew where she was going. *She* knew why she was doing what she was doing. What did it matter what one passing stranger out of the hundreds thought of her?

'Like it?' Dominic murmured lazily. 'Think you might want to refute it?'

'I don't have to refute anything to *you*, but let me just tell you that I'm not an easy lay.' Understatement of the century, she was honest enough to think. One lover in all her years. Frankie King, whom she had known since she was sixteen. And she hadn't even slept with him for…how many months now?

'So if that's why you followed me, then you can forget it. I won't be climbing into your bed, not now, not ever.'

A mixed group of merry teenagers, drunk but too wrapped up in each other to be threatening to her, jostled past and Dominic took hold of her arm and led her away from the ticket machines to the side.

'I'll take you home in a taxi.'

'Oh, suddenly a little bit scared of our great British transport system, are you?' she sneered, not much liking the way she sounded. Hard and jaded and cynical, but this was the best way she knew of protecting herself.

'Oh, don't be such a damned little fool.'

'Well, it might interest you to know that I'd rather take my chances with that little lot that just waltzed past than cooped up in a taxi with you.'

'Then I'll just put you in the damned cab and pay the man to take you wherever it is you live!'

'Ah. Not so keen on my company now that you know I won't be sleeping with you.' Mattie shook her head with an expression of mock disappointment. 'Now, why am I not falling down in surprise?'

'Come on.' He had never met a more suspicious, cynical woman in his life, but did she have spirit! Was that why he was now hailing a taxi for her rather than letting her take the first tube of the morning home? Not liking the thought of her stepping into a carriage with a mob of drunks, even though she was right and was probably more accustomed to dealing with situations like that than he was?

'You, mister, are the last word in arrogance!'

'Watch out. I might start getting used to your line of compliments.'

'Hardly.' The black cab had slowed down for her and she knew better than to kick up her heels at his insistence. 'Unless fate decides to behave in a freakish way, this is the last we'll be seeing of each other.'

Dominic didn't say anything. Just opened the taxi door for her, handed the driver some notes, sufficient, he was assured, to cover the trip, before turning to her briefly.

His large, powerful frame was draped suffocatingly by her open door, and when he looked down at her his presence seemed to fill the entire back of the taxi like a drug.

'Oh, I don't think so,' he said in a low, silky voice, and Mattie felt a disturbing thread of excitement race up her spine. 'After all, I have yet to refute your accusations, do I not?'

'I apologise,' she said quickly. 'There. Will that do?'

'I'll see you tomorrow.'

'I'll never sleep with you,' she hissed fiercely. 'You've got the wrong measure of me!'

'In life, I've learnt that *never* is the most fickle word in the English language.' With which he stood up and slammed the car door.

What he didn't tell her was that it was also the most challenging word in the English language. Especially in this context and especially for a man like him.

CHAPTER TWO

'DUNNO know why you bother wasting your time on that rubbish.'

Mattie glanced across the room to Frankie. He was sprawled on the chair in front of the television, his feet propped up on the coffee-table he had dragged over, and he was staring at her in a way that she was all too familiar with.

So she ignored him and returned to the books in front of her. 'Told you, love, there's no way you've got the brains to do anything in any company anywhere. Left school at sixteen, or you forgotten already?'

He was on the beer. For that she was grateful. If he had been on the whisky, he would be targeting his comments with a lot more venom. And he would be gone in a little while. It was Saturday, after all. Not a night for a man like Frankie to stay in. Not when his mates would be down at the local, eyes glued to whatever sport happened to be showing on the massive overhead screen that The Lamb and Eagle proudly sported.

'That doesn't mean I can't do this,' Mattie said quietly, knowing that there was no point going down this road but doing it anyway.

'Sure it does. Big shots in companies ain't looking for a girl like you, Mats. Pretty you might be but let's not forget the background.' He gave a cruel little chuckle and her fingers tightened on the pen she was holding. 'Anyway, what time you off tonight, then?'

'Does it matter? You won't be here anyway.'

'True, true. Go and fetch us another beer, would you, Mats?'

'You'll be drinking at the pub, Frankie.'

'Oh not another of your little preachy sermons. Don't think I can stand it. Any wonder I want to clear out of this place whenever you're around? A right little Miss Prim and Proper you've become ever since you started filling your head with ideas about high-flying jobs in marketing. You should 'ave just stuck it out as secretary in that poxy little company you were at before.'

Pushed to the limit, Mattie snapped shut the book she had been studying and fixed him with a cold stare.

'But I couldn't, could I, Frankie? And we both know why!'

He staggered to his feet, raked his fingers through his hair and headed towards the kitchen with a thunderous scowl on his face. But this time she wasn't going to let him get away with his jibe.

Three nights ago it had felt damned good to yell at someone and she was going to do that now. This time at the right person instead of at a perfect stranger who had happened to rub her up the wrong way. A perfect stranger who had, unsurprisingly, not reappeared at her exciting little workplace, even though she had caught herself watching out for him, and then berating herself for letting him get under her skin when she had figured him out for what he was.

'Well?' Mattie went to the kitchen door and leaned against the frame, her eyes stormy, watching as Frankie helped himself to another lager, which he proceeded to drink straight from the can.

'I can't be bothered to argue this one with you, Mats. Why don't you just head back to those books of yours and carry on pretending you can get somewhere in life?'

'No! I want to have this one out, Frankie. I'm sick to death of all your slurs and insults. I couldn't stick it out in that job because the money wasn't enough to keep us both!' She had tiptoed round this long enough.

'I suppose you blame me for the accident!'

'I don't blame you for anything! But that was nearly two years ago! So isn't it about time you just woke up to the fact that you will *never* become a professional footballer? It's over, Frankie! You need to get your head around that and—'

'Know what, Mats? I don't need to stand here and listen to all of this! I'm off.'

She felt tears of frustration prick the backs of her eyes, but she stayed where she was, blocking the doorway.

'You need to get a job, Frankie.'

He slammed the half-empty beer can on the kitchen table and lager shot out of the top over the table-top.

'An office job, Mats? Think I should get myself decked out in a cheap suit and see if anyone wants me?'

'It doesn't have to be an office job.'

'Well, then, maybe a job like yours, then, eh?'

'That job happens to pay five times what I was getting as a secretary and a hundred times more than I was getting working at that restaurant.'

'So you could take time off and study those books of yours. As if you'll ever be able to do anything in any company.'

'Well, it didn't last long, did it? I had to jack that in so that I could get something better paid to pay the bills *you* have no intention of paying because you won't get a job!'

'Know what? If you feel that way, why don't you just clear off, Mats?' His blue eyes met hers and he looked away.

'Maybe I will,' she said, turning away, only half hearing him as he apologised. Again. Told her he needed her. Again. Slammed his way out of the house. Again.

They both knew that the end of their relationship had already arrived, had arrived quite some time ago, as it happened. But Mattie knew how hard it was to say goodbye to history, to memories of them both as teenagers, when they had had high hopes of going places. Just as she knew that the only glue keeping them together, as far as she was concerned anyway, was pity.

His star had been so promising, and then when the accident happened she had just felt so damned sorry for him, too sorry to take the final step and walk away even though she could see how he had changed, how they both had.

He was enraged and bitter at what fate had done to him but even those spells of anguish, of opening up to her, communicating, had dwindled away. She realised that they hadn't really communicated in months.

Not, she thought as she tidied away her books and began getting dressed to leave the house, since he had broken down and sobbed like a baby on her shoulder over eight months ago. When yet again she had allowed herself to feel sorry for him, to struggle on with him, knowing that he needed her.

She had, after all, known him for such a long time.

In a way, the nightclub was just the right job for her, quite aside from the fantastic earnings.

There was no time to think about her own problems when she was busy scuttling around the tables, catching up with the other girls now and again so that they could share a giggle about their customers.

But their argument tonight had been different. Had had an edge to it that they had both felt.

Two hours later her mind was still harking back to it, when she looked up and there he was, the man, the stranger, sitting on his own at the back of the room, and her heart gave a sudden, illogical leap of pleasure which disappeared as fast as it had come.

How long had he been sitting there?

And now that she had spotted him, she became acutely conscious of her every movement until finally she had no choice but to walk towards him, even though he wasn't seated in her patch.

'What are *you* doing here?'

'I told you I would return,' he asked with the same slightly amused, lazy drawl that sent a shiver up her spine. 'Missed me?'

'Of course I haven't *missed* you, and I also thought I'd made my position clear. I'm not for sale along with the drinks and the food.' And, since there was no more to be said on the subject, she knew that she should just spin round on her heel and walk away, leaving him ample time to get the message once and for all. But she didn't. She hesitated.

'Why don't we leave here and go somewhere a little more civilised for some coffee? I know a particularly good coffee bar that's open all hours.'

'A coffee bar that's open all hours? Oh, please! And where would that be? On another planet?'

'Actually, in a hotel that caters for men like me. Not, I might add, the lying pervert you categorised me as but a workaholic who keeps highly irregular hours.' He raised one eyebrow, leaned back into his chair and proceeded to watch her very intently.

'I don't think so. Thanks all the same.'

'You look exhausted.'

Three words that made her stop in her tracks, brought

back the flood of memories of what had taken place between her and Frankie. Right now, there wasn't a nook or cranny in her life that wasn't exhausting. How had he spotted that when no one else had?

'There are one or two reasons why that's totally out of the question,' Mattie said tartly. 'And if you choose to disregard the ones I've already given you, then here are a couple more. I've only been here for an hour and a half and this is my job. Sorry.'

'It occurred to me,' Dominic said, sweeping past her little speech as if it was of no consequence, 'that I don't even know your name. What is it?'

'Look. I have to go. Jackie will hit the roof if she thinks I'm muscling in on her customers.'

'Why do you work in a place like this?'

'I already told you. Now, goodbye.'

'I'll meet you at the exit in half an hour.' He stood up, finished his drink and looked down at her. 'Right?'

'I'm not going anywhere with you! How much does it take to get through that thick skull of yours?'

'I'll sort it out with your boss.'

Mattie gave a short, dry laugh. 'Oh, right. And how do you propose to do that? Put a gun to his head, by any chance?'

'I've always found that strong-arm tactics never work.' His dark eyes locked with hers and he felt that sudden surge of unexplained excitement once again. The same excitement that had coursed through him whenever she crossed his mind. Which she had done with puzzling regularity over the past few days.

Why? Logic told him that if all he wanted was a safe and enjoyable antidote to Rosalind, then he could find that anywhere. He certainly didn't need to pursue a woman who had made her feelings patently clear from the word go. But logic was no match for what he could only put down to the thrill of a challenge, and challenge, he had grudgingly admitted, was certainly what she was.

Hence his reason for returning to the nightclub.

'Leave it to me.'

Leave it to him! Well, why not? He didn't know Harry and he obviously had no idea how strict nightclub bosses were when it came to their girls not skipping off work.

'Sure.' She shot him a caustic grin. 'If you can pull that one off, then I'll come with you to your coffee bar, by all means. But, since I don't see that happening, I'll just bid you goodnight and tell you that it's no use your coming back here because the next time you won't even get a conversation out of me.'

It was a little disconcerting to feel a tug of regret at the thought of that, but Mattie was nothing if not practical. Her life was just too full of problems for her to take another one on board in the shape of a man, probably married, because good-looking, well-spoken men like that were never single, who was after a little no-strings-attached fling with a pretty young thing.

She would make sure not to look in his direction again.

What she hadn't bargained on was Harry calling her over ten minutes later as she was on her way back for a refill of champagne for a table of men who had already had far too much to drink.

'I *what*?' Mattie stammered, after he had said what he had to say.

'Can take the rest of the evening off.'

'I've just got here, Harry.'

'Jacks won't mind covering your patch. She needs to catch up on some lost earnings.'

'How did he do it?' Mattie glanced around her, seeking him out in the darkness and through the crowds, then finally returning her narrowed eyes to Harry's flushed face. 'Well?' she demanded. Then a thought crossed her mind. 'He didn't…he isn't…*some kind of dangerous thug,* is he, Harry? He didn't *threaten* you, did he?' She thought back to her throw-away remark about guns and heads.

'Threaten *me*? Harry Alfonso Roberto Sidwell?' He rocked on the balls of his feet for a few seconds, straightened the lapels of his jacket and gave her a superior look. 'No one has ever dared do such a thing, Matilda Hayes, and don't you forget it! No. Just said he wanted to talk to you, that this seemed the only time you could snatch. Gave me his card. Told me that if I ever needed any advice, just ask for him.'

'Advice? Advice about what?' She felt as if the ground had unexpectedly opened up from under her feet. 'Relationships? Is he some kind of counsellor or something?'

'Harry Sidwell has *never* needed advice on relationships! He's in finance, Mats. Powerful man. Even *I've* heard of him and you know how much distance there is between the underbelly of life here and the Olympic heights of some of those money men.' He chuckled at his own sense of humour but Mattie's head was reeling with shock.

'*You're giving me the night off because some man asked you to and handed over a business card?* And *what about my tips*, Harry? I can't afford to take the time off! You know how much I need the money!'

'I'll cover you, Mats. Give you roughly the amount you usually pull in on a Friday. Don't say I'm not fair.'

'I can't—'

'You deserve a night off, Mattie. Reliable as clockwork, you are. Never let me down. When was the last time you went out for enjoyment? Eh? When you're not at college or poring over textbooks, you're here. And you'd be doing me a favour, love.'

'How's that, Harry?'

'Thinking of expanding business, Mats. Might need that business card sooner than you think.' He grinned craftily, and Mattie felt her options closing in.

'He's after one thing, Harry. Thanks very much!'

'You're safe with that one.'

'I wouldn't be safe with *anybody* who comes here, and you know it!'

'You're safe with that one, Mats. I wouldn't be giving you the evening off otherwise. He's a big cheese. He wouldn't make a nuisance of himself because he's too high-profile. Would never risk a scandal. If he says he wants to talk, then that's all he'll do. Unless…'

'Unless *what*?'

'Unless you decide otherwise…'

'Fat chance.'

'Then what's the problem? Free evening? Enjoy yourself. Now, you go change, darling. Busy, busy, busy here tonight. No time to stop and have a prolonged chat.'

But she didn't like the feeling of being manipulated. Even if it did feel good to have an evening to herself. No books, no nightclub. No Frankie.

If she got to the door and discovered that he had changed his mind, all the better. She'd play truant and skip one evening's work and find herself some twenty-four-hour place where she could just sit and be at peace with her thoughts. Going back to the house was not an option, even though Frankie wouldn't be there. Just being within those four walls was enough to make her feel suffocated.

But he was there. Waiting. Just as he had promised. Tall, impossibly handsome and looking at her with an expression she couldn't read, which made her feel more apprehensive rather than less. Apprehensive and some-how...*alert*. Alive.

'How did you pull that off?' was the first thing she asked, glaring.

Like an angry cat, he thought. An angry cat that he had got it into his head he wanted to tame. An angry cat that would jump six feet into the air if he so much as touched her, even if the touch was strictly polite. He pushed open the door and stood back so that she could brush past him.

'Didn't Harry tell you?' Dominic asked curiously, making sure not to invade her space.

'He said you gave him your business card. He said you were someone important in the City.' Mattie re-garded him levelly, with hostile suspicion. 'I don't care how important you are, you know the ground rules.'

'But not your name.'

'Sorry?'

'I know the ground rules, but I still don't know your name.'

'Matilda.'

'Matilda. You don't look like a Matilda,' he said in an amused voice, and her back stiffened.

'No. And what do I look like? Something a little fluff-ier? A Candy, perhaps? Maybe fluffier still?'

'Are you always on the defensive? Matilda?'

'Mattie,' Mattie muttered. 'Everyone calls me Mattie. I hate the name Matilda.' She blushed at this unneces-sary volunteering of information, even though it was hardly a state secret.

'Why?'

She shrugged, as he knew she would, just as he knew that she hated having let slip the innocuous detail because it was of a personal nature.

'Well, Mattie,' he stretched out one arm to hail a taxi, and as it slowed down to pull up to them he said with deadly seriousness, 'we're going to have to get in a cab together to go to this hotel…'

'Hotel? Oh, no. No, no.' She began backing away and Dominic clicked his tongue in impatience.

'I said *hotel*. I didn't say *hotel room*. We're going to a hotel in Covent Garden that I often use when I'm working late. There's a bar downstairs and it's guaranteed to be full.' But her big green eyes were still watching him warily, and he had to fight the urge to just reach out and smooth her ruffled feathers.

He, who had never had to try when it came to the opposite sex, could scarcely believe that he was now willing, at some ungodly time of the evening, to bide his time.

'Now, are you going to come with me or not? If not, then you can rest assured that you won't see me again. If you do decide to come, then you'll just have to swallow your misgivings and climb into this taxi with me. Make your mind up.'

He saw the debate flitting across her face and wondered what he would do if she walked away. Wondered what had brought him to this juncture in the first place.

Fate? A certain boredom with the women he was used to? A need to erase Rosalind by having an affair with someone dramatically different from her in every possible way? Something else? No, nothing else, he told himself.

But whatever the outcome of her internal debate, he wasn't going to chase after her. He had already behaved out of character as far as she was concerned, and he wasn't going to do it again.

'OK.' Mattie shrugged and, when she reached out to open the door, found that he was there before her, opening it for her. It was a gesture to which she wasn't accustomed. Frankie was not an opening-car-doors-for-women kind of man.

Still, she made sure to wriggle up to the furthest side of the seat when he stooped to join her, and was immediately glad of it because, even at this distance, she still felt chokingly aware of him.

'I don't know your name,' she said, as the taxi pulled away.

He noticed the way she was huddled against the door, as if scared that he might do something unexpected at any given moment, and he, in turn, made sure to keep a safe distance between them.

'Dominic Drecos.'

'Dominic Drecos,' Mattie repeated, thinking hard. 'And you're something important in the City, are you?'

'Something important, yes.' She didn't sound overly impressed with that and he found himself giving in to a childish desire to expand. 'I deal in corporate finance. We handle mergers and acquisitions. In addition, I speculate in property. Buy to renovate to sell.'

'Right.' She turned to gaze out of the window. In this part of London, it was never dark. Too many lights and billboards. It was a rolling scenery she was familiar with, but for some reason she found it easier to stare at the images moving past than at the man sitting on the seat next to her.

He was the first man she had had a proper conversation with in a very long time. She attended her courses during the day but did none of the student socialising that most of the others did and talking to the customers at the nightclub was strictly out of the question. There had just been Frankie. And she and Frankie no longer conversed on any meaningful level.

'So you don't live here, then, I take it?' She reluctantly looked at him and, for one crazy moment, wondered what he looked like underneath the expensive suit and that crisp striped shirt he was wearing under it. Then she blinked and she was back in the taxi, a nightclub waitress with a boyfriend, sitting next to someone important in the City.

'Why do you say that?'

'Well, if you did, then why would you go to a hotel when you happened to be working late?'

'I have an apartment in Chelsea. But this particular hotel does very late suppers and occasionally we might come across here to wind up a deal and eat at the same time.'

'We?'

'My people.'

'Your people.'

'Accountants, lawyers, whoever happens to be needed. Sometimes, I come here on my own to have a late meal and finish business without the distraction of telephones and fax machines.' No point telling her that he had been responsible for buying and renovating this particular building and, as a stipulation, had a penthouse suite on the top floor which he sometimes used if he simply couldn't be bothered to get George to drive him back to his own apartment. That little titbit would have her running for cover.

And he was discovering that the last thing he wanted was to have her running for cover.

For someone who had always had total control over

every aspect of his life, this in itself puzzled the hell out of him. It also energised him in equal measure.

'And what about your wife? Does she enjoy your late suppers at expensive hotels when you're working late with your people?' Whether he was married or not was immaterial to her. She had no intention of doing anything with him. But she still found that she was curious.

Was he married?

'If I were married, I wouldn't be here.' There was a flat coolness to his voice that made her want to retract the question. 'Don't you find it impossible to work somewhere where your opinion of your customers is so low?'

She was spared the difficulty of finding an answer to that one by the taxi slowing down in front of an elegant building sandwiched between an expensive men's clothing shop and a furniture shop that sported chic, very modern, unpriced handmade furniture.

But somehow she got the feeling that the question would be repeated the minute they were on their own.

In the meantime, she would take some time to get her thoughts together and try to still the fluttery feeling in the pit of her stomach that definitely should not be there.

'Not the sort of place for a girl in jeans,' she whispered with a nervous laugh as they walked into the foyer. Stark colours, one or two abstract paintings on the walls, plants that seemed to make a statement.

And he had been right. There were people even in the foyer, even at this hour of the night. Expensive, sophisticated, arty-looking people.

The man behind the desk smiled at him, which just made Mattie feel even more nervous. She clenched her fists in the pockets of her jacket and trudged alongside him as he strode towards some stairs and down into the basement bar.

What was she doing here? she wondered a little wildly.

'People come here dressed in anything they choose,' Dominic murmured down to her. 'No need to feel out of place.'

'I wasn't feeling out of place.'

'No?' He paused to raise one eyebrow at her, and she smiled reluctantly.

'Well, a little.'

It was the smile, he thought. Something about it gave the lie to her air of cynicism, revealed a wealth of vulnerability and spoke volumes about the wit, the humour, the intelligence lying there just below the surface. Waiting.

Waiting, he thought, for me to unearth it.

'Grab a table,' he said. 'I'll get drinks. What will you have?'

'Not champagne. I see enough of that at work to be immune to its charm. Not that I've ever been a champagne girl anyway,' she added quickly, just in case he thought that she was going to take advantage of his wealth to order herself the most expensive drink on the menu. 'I'll have some coffee, please. Decaffeinated, if they do it.'

'They do everything here.'

Mattie took a seat at one of the smooth circular granite tables. The chairs were oddly shaped, very comfortable even though they didn't look it, and, as in the foyer, there were people here. A whole world of night birds, exotic, young night birds, drinking and having a good time.

'So,' he deposited her cup on the table and sat down, 'feeling a little less…rattled?'

'I wasn't rattled,' Mattie returned with vigour. 'I was angry because you manipulated me into leaving with you.'

'You could have said no and walked away. No one forced you to get into the taxi and come here.' He crossed his legs and proceeded to look at her with such thoroughness that she felt a steady blush invade her face until she was taking refuge in the cup of coffee and wishing she had ordered something a little more substantial.

'And you never answered my question. Why do you work in a place where the customers obviously repulse you?'

'They don't repulse me. Some of them are really quite nice. Or at least they seem to be.'

'You just dislike the sort of men you think frequent those places.'

'Wouldn't you?' Mattie shrugged, determined not to let him see how nervously aware of him he made her feel.

'Funnily enough, I feel exactly the same as you do. I just happened to find myself there at the request of my clients.'

'Oh, and you weren't enjoying…having a look around?'

'Not particularly. Until, that is, I saw you.'

There was something shockingly direct about the statement, something that made her body stir slickly into life. She couldn't think of a thing to say and nor did he seem in any hurry to break the silence that thickened around them.

'I…I… As I said, I work there because the money is very good… I…'

Dominic watched as she lowered her eyes and busied herself with the cup, staring at it for a few seconds, toying with the handle before raising it to her lips. She was probably as experienced as they came, but she was making him feel like a big, bad wolf all of a sudden and he didn't like the feeling.

'Why don't you get a day job?' he asked, allowing the change of subject even though he wanted to ask her how she could possibly do what she did and still shy away like a frightened rabbit when a man paid her a compliment. He hadn't even tried to touch her, for heaven's sake!

'Why is it that you aren't married?' She tilted her chin up and looked him squarely in the face, leaving him in no doubt as to her intention. If he felt at liberty to quiz her about her private life then she felt at liberty to do the same to him.

'Should I be?' Dominic hedged. Personal confidences had never figured high on his conversational agenda. Had never figured at all, in point of fact. He felt his face darken slightly and he knocked back the remainder of his drink in one long swallow.

'Well, you're not too old, you're…you're…' Her vantage point was quickly relinquished as Mattie saw the road she was heading down. A list of all his credentials, and when she looked at him there was a wicked gleam in his eyes that did something else to her wall of cynicism that had been so carefully erected over the years.

'I'm all ears,' he encouraged.

'Obviously rich. Being something big in the City, as you are.'

'Anything else?'

'Yes. Arrogant. Manipulative. Oh, not forgetting, with an ego as big as a tanker.'

'Mmm. Doesn't sound a list of qualities any woman would positively search for.'

Their eyes tangled and Mattie was the first to look away. The conversation was getting dangerous. Some little voice was telling her that.

'Which just shows that you probably haven't met the right one,' she said quickly. 'So how did you discover this place?' she asked, making no attempt to hide the change of subject.

'Oh, I bought the building, renovated it and then sold it on.' He watched her digest this information whilst his mind began to drift off into images of that exotically beautiful face glowing with the film of passion, her body unclothed, writhing in a lover's embrace. His embrace.

He cleared his throat, sat up straighter. 'As I mentioned, that's a part of what I do.'

She found she wanted to hear more. Wanted to find out more about him. It wouldn't do. Time to rectify a situation before it became too dangerous.

'Sounds very important. So…how did you manage to just land up doing that? It must cost an absolute fortune to go into the property business. Mustn't it? Especially in London.'

'I studied economics at university,' Dominic said abruptly. 'Went into finance before I got into the property side.'

'You must have made a great deal of money in finance in that case. To enable you to have the capital to play with.' Mattie pretended to muse on the conundrum of this.

Dominic gave her a long, narrowed look which she

met with widely innocent eyes. 'I've always had a fair amount of money at my disposal.'

'Ah.' Of course he would have. He was a man born into money. It sat on his shoulders like an invisible cloak. And she had wanted him to say it. Out loud. So that she could remind herself of yet another reason why she should get out of this place and fast, before his sexy face and ability to listen and smooth-talking charm got the better of her caution.

'So…what did your parents do?'

'Is this really relevant?'

'It is to me.'

'My father is in shipping.'

'Builds them, you mean?'

'You know exactly what I mean.'

'My mum was a cleaner. She died ten years ago. My dad was a carpenter, except not many people seem to want handmade things these days. He lives in Bournemouth now. He still makes bits and pieces for himself, but his full-time job is supervisor at a furniture factory.' Mattie stood up and smiled politely.

She felt disproportionately hurt at the fact that she would never see him again, but she had had to do it. Had to make him see the one difference between them that would always be there.

'Well, thanks for the coffee. No, please, I can get a taxi home myself.' She just couldn't face the underground just now. And before he could say another word she was hurrying out of the door, up the stairs and through the chic foyer that looked as though it had stepped straight out of a magazine.

CHAPTER THREE

'OH, NO, you don't.'

Mattie heard the rapid footsteps behind her at the same time as she heard his voice, which was just as he gripped her arm and swung her around to face him.

'You are *not* going to sling this in my face and then run away before I have time to refute it.'

'I'm not running away from anything. I'm going home, if it's all the same to you!'

'No, well, as a matter of fact, it's not.'

Her heart was beating a mile a minute, racing inside her like a roller coaster that had gone wildly out of control, and his hand on her arm was like a vice grip, but one that was doing crazy things to her stomach, just the sort of crazy things she didn't want to happen.

'Well, tough!'

'Not good enough, Mattie.' He reached out one hand to hail a taxi and kept the other one firmly on her arm. 'Where do you live? I'll drop you home. We can talk on the way.'

'No!'

Drop her home? And what if Frankie just happened to be up and moving around? Unlikely, but not a possibility she could rule out. Frankie, after a few bottles of beer, couldn't be relied on to behave in a predictable manner and go to sleep. And the thought of him storming out of the house and confronting Dominic Drecos was enough to make her blood curdle. She knew who would be the loser and it wouldn't be the man opening the door of the taxi now for her to step past him.

'Why not?' Dominic demanded, leaning forward, invading her space and noticing that she was leaning forward too, not shrinking away from him like a scared rabbit.

'Because…'

'Because what?'

'Because…' Because she didn't want Frankie, if he happened to be up, to see her with him? To get the wrong idea? Because even after all they had been through, she still didn't have it in her to hurt him like that? Or was it, she wondered uneasily, because she didn't want this man to know that a boyfriend existed?

'Because I don't reveal my address to strangers, especially when those strangers happen to have been a customer in the nightclub where I work!'

Dominic grimaced, seeing her point of view but knowing that the last thing he would do would be to take advantage of her. He had covered some distance, he thought with another grimace to himself, since he had first set eyes on her and concluded that he wanted her. Now, along with those signals that she sent out, that had every masculine pore in his body rearing into full-blooded life, were other, more complex ones. He wanted to get to know her, against all his better judgement, and in order to do that he would have to take his time.

'In which case, I suggest we go back to my apartment.'

Mattie almost laughed at the suggestion, even though a treacherous part of her stirred at the thought of it.

'Over my dead body.'

'Where there is a very comfortable sitting area downstairs. We can finish our conversation.' He gave his address to the taxi driver and was aware of her staring at him for having removed the decision from her hands.

'You really have got a nerve! How dare you?'

'Stop running from me,' he drawled softly. 'I always catch the things I want, Mattie.'

'And you want me.'

'And I want you.'

He wasn't touching her, but God, she felt her body burn as if he were.

'You want a good-looking waitress in a nightclub. You don't want *me*. You don't *even know me*.'

'Is that a plea from the heart?' he drawled.

'It's a matter-of-fact statement, actually,' Mattie snapped in return. 'You may have spent your life with women tripping behind you in your wake, wondering if they might be the lucky little thing to get the ring on her finger, but, *buddy*, where I come from I can see straight through men like you! You're a taker, Mr Drecos.'

'But you don't *even know me*.'

Mattie uttered the strangled sound of someone whose impeccable reason has been neatly lobbed right back at them, and decided that she wouldn't dignify his comment with a reply. Not that she could think of anything to say to his barbed piece of verbal cleverness.

But she didn't like the fact that she was sitting in a taxi with him and being transported to wherever his apartment was, even though that gut feeling she had had three evenings before was back with her. A deep knowing that he was a man who didn't lie. If he said that there would be somewhere downstairs where they could talk, then there would be.

The problem was that she didn't want to talk.

No, she amended truthfully to herself, the problem

was that she was a little too tempted to talk for her own good.

She felt as though her emotions had been put on hold forever, building up behind a dam which was beginning to strain at the weight put against it.

She wanted to talk, but why him? He had already told her what kind of interest he was feeling and it wasn't the sort that wanted to get to know her, whatever he had to say on the subject. It was the sort that wanted to get her into his bed.

'If I get there and I find that the only thing waiting downstairs is a lift to carry me up to your apartment, then you're out of luck. I'll walk straight back out of the door and into the nearest taxi I can find!'

'Fair enough.'

He had deprived her of further argument, but he could still feel her simmering away next to him. Sexy as hell and as appealingly defensive as a cornered cat.

He watched her averted profile, the stubborn tilt of her head, and wondered if she had any idea how seductive her mutinous silence was.

By the time the taxi pulled up in front of his apartment block, he was almost willing to bet that she would have changed her mind about coming in.

But all she said to the driver was, 'Would you mind waiting here for a few minutes? Just in case I need to get back to my house?'

'No problem, love.'

'Well? Does it pass muster?' Dominic asked, the minute they were inside the building. 'There's the sitting area over there and, as you can see, there's a security guy permanently on call by the desk. His name's Charlie and I'm sure he'll fly to your rescue if you decide to start shrieking.'

'Very funny.'

'So are you going to tell our taxi driver to disappear or are you going to climb into his taxi and run away again?'

It was his implication of cowardice that did it. Or so Mattie told herself. She walked out of the foyer without answering, leaving him to nurse the unsettling thought that she had decided to clear off, then returned almost immediately.

Dominic could hardly believe the surge of relief that washed over him.

They stood and stared at one another, across the expanse of expensively tiled foyer, with Charlie's curious gaze flicking from one to the other, and Mattie was the first to move, walking towards him with the same wary expression on her face.

'Would you like something to drink?'

'Where from? I don't see too many vending machines around here.'

'No vending machines,' Dominic agreed, standing perfectly still, waiting for her to approach him, to look up at him. 'But a kitchen just off behind you. Charlie has all the necessary equipment to provide us with coffee or tea or whatever your preference is. At a pinch, he could probably rustle up something to eat, although I wouldn't guarantee that it would go beyond a sandwich.'

'Coffee would be fine.'

'And you can take your jacket off,' Dominic said drily. 'Sit wherever you like.'

Unlike many London apartment blocks, this particular one was fairly unique in so far as there was always a porter manning a desk at the front, and the actual hall area was extensive. Large enough to accommodate the generous proportions of Charlie's desk, as well as two separate sets of sitting areas and a fair number of plants that were cleaned and watered daily.

She was still standing uncertainly when he returned to her with two mugs of coffee and a plate of biscuits balanced precariously on the top of one of the mugs.

'This is beautiful,' Mattie said politely, following his lead and sitting down, though not on the two-seater sofa alongside him, but in the chair facing him.

He was at home here. He breathed power and wealth and these surroundings were tailor-made for men who were powerful and wealthy. The marble tiles on the floor gleamed, the brass details on the balustrade that wound up the flights of stairs were indecently shiny, the overhead chandeliers were solid and impressive.

'So.' She sipped some of the coffee and tried to remain blithely underwhelmed by the surroundings. 'You have an apartment here...'

'I have...'

She could sense his dark eyes fixed on her as she slowly looked all around and had never felt more self-conscious in her life before. Jeans, a sweatshirt and trainers were not at home in a place like this, although, in all fairness, he hardly seemed to notice her attire.

She noticed, though, and weakly reminded herself that her duty was to carry on pointing out all the differences between them, as she had started to do in the hotel bar.

'So...you live in London, full-time. Do you?'

'I live primarily in London, but I travel a lot.'

'Oh, yes. Of course. To visit your parents in Greece, I expect.'

'Among other things.'

'What other things?'

'Work, usually. New York, Paris. Just recently, the Middle East.'

'Leading eventually to what? A global takeover?' She laughed a little nervously and sipped some more of the coffee. 'It all sounds very high-powered. And what do you do when you want to relax? Nightclubs?'

'When I want to relax, I usually go to the Cotswolds. I have a house there. If you perch any closer on the edge of that chair, you're going to fall off.'

Mattie wriggled into a more comfortable position. 'You have a house in the Cotswolds. A country retreat.'

'Something like that.' The look he gave her was one of gleaming, devilish amusement. 'Now, aren't you going to attack me for the luxury?'

She shrugged. 'I wasn't attacking you earlier on, if that's what you're implying.'

'No? What were you doing, in that case?'

'I was reminding you why you don't stand a chance in hell of getting me into your bed, never mind your big-headed notion that whatever you want in life you get.'

'Why don't you come and sit here next to me on this sofa and tell me that again?'

It was like being shot through with a volt of electricity that ran from the tips of her toes to the hair on her scalp, but she made herself look at him with incredulity.

'Is that how you would address the women you go out with?' she fired scornfully.

'No, I don't suppose it is.'

'I know that. Because I happen to work in a nightclub, you think that you can speak to me just as you want to and poor, awestruck little me would have no choice but to immediately fall to my feet!'

'Because the women I go out with would already have taken the decision to sit right here next to me. If, of course, we were here in the first place.'

The implication in his lazy statement rushed at her and reddened her face.

No, he wouldn't be sitting in the foyer here when his apartment was only an elevator ride away.

'Would you be as defensive as you are if we hadn't met in a nightclub?' he asked curiously. 'If I didn't know what you did for a living?'

'We wouldn't have met.'

'You haven't answered my question.'

'I'm not defensive,' Mattie lied and prevaricated at the same time. 'I'm a realist. We come from opposite sides of the tracks. Look at the way you're dressed, for heaven's sake! I would bet my life that that suit of yours wasn't sitting on a peg in a department store on Oxford Street. Was it?'

'This line of conversation isn't going to get us anywhere.'

'I don't *want* to *get* anywhere with you!'

'Then why are you here?'

Mattie flushed. 'Because I was manipulated into coming,' she said awkwardly.

'Don't be ridiculous. Now you're pretending to be a passive victim of circumstance. Is that how you feel? About being here? With me? About yourself?'

'You don't understand.'

'Try me.'

'I want to go home now.'

'No, you don't. Come upstairs to my apartment. It's more comfortable than being down here.'

'More dangerous, you mean.'

'Do you think I'm dangerous?'

'A girl can't be too careful.'

'Do you?'

'I wasn't born yesterday, Mr Drecos.'

'Stop calling me that. The name is Dominic. And you still haven't answered my question.'

'You've already told me what your intentions are.'

'I've never gone near a woman who didn't want me to be near her. Let's go upstairs.'

'I'll stay half an hour then I'm off. And this time, I don't want you coming back to the nightclub to see me! OK?'

He didn't answer. Instead, he stood up, waiting for her, giving her time to consider what she had done. Going upstairs with him to his apartment! Another step towards the edge of a cliff, or that was how she felt.

Although, she told herself sternly, hadn't she made sure to tell him that, after tonight, no more?

She walked with him to the lift and concentrated hard on the control panel as they were whirred up and the doors opened to a lushly carpeted corridor.

She knew that his apartment was going to be luxurious. But she wasn't prepared for exactly how luxurious.

Rich wooden floors peppered with silky Persian rugs, an open-plan layout that exaggerated the space and allowed the eye to roam freely over the beautiful spread of low, clean-lined furniture, glass-topped dining-table with a thick band of wood framing the glass, white walls interrupted with large, dramatic paintings. And the kitchen, to which he was now heading, was simply separated from the rest of the open space by a large semi-circular, granite-topped counter.

Mattie watched him, the way he dominated every inch of his surroundings, and felt another shiver of alarm that he had managed to get her this far.

'Like it?' he asked, fiddling with a high-tech coffee machine, and she licked her lips nervously and then sat on one of the chrome and wooden high stools at the kitchen counter.

'Who wouldn't?'

'Where do you live?' He slid a plain, squat, white china mug over to her and then perched on a similar stool to face her across the counter.

This was what she had dreaded. The intimacy of being somewhere private with him, and it couldn't get more private than this, but his remark about her seeing herself as a passive victim had rankled and had been one of the reasons she had agreed to come up here with him. She could take control.

'Privileged information, I'm afraid.' They were both leaning on the counter, holding their mugs to their lips, and their eyes met.

She had a face, he thought, looking at her, that he quite simply enjoyed watching. It wasn't just the beauty of the features or the luminosity of her green eyes or the way her silver-blonde hair cascaded down her back. It was the humour and intelligence he could see there which she tried so hard to conceal underneath an aggressive hostility that seemed at odds with the physical look she presented.

She had a mind that he enjoyed tussling with.

And she had thrown him a gauntlet that he couldn't resist taking up.

'Now, I wonder why I shouldn't have guessed that,' he drawled, sipping his coffee and looking at her over the rim of his cup. 'What do you do when you're not working?'

'Why?'

'Because, generally speaking, these are the sorts of things two people might ask one another in the course of conversation.'

Mattie considered the question and tried to work out why she was finding this man so disconcerting. However, since she wasn't going to be seeing him again after tonight, what was the point in concealing what she had no reason to hide?

'I try and grab some sleep whenever I can.'

'How long have you been there?'

'Oh, about seven or eight months.'

She was still looking at him cautiously with those amazing eyes, as if she expected him to make some sudden move and was braced to defend herself.

She had relaxed enough to take her jacket off, though, and had shoved up the sleeves of her jumper so that her slender arms were exposed, lightly dusted with golden hair. Her watch was a cheap plastic affair with a thick pink strap.

She was right when she said that they came from opposite sides of the tracks. Rosalind, for starters, would never have been seen dead without her delicate gold Rolex.

He caught himself and remembered that this was not intended to be a relationship, but an affair in the making. He was, he reminded himself, through with relationships.

'And before that?'

Mattie shrugged. 'Oh, I worked in a restaurant.'

'So you sleep by day and work by night. A vampire's existence.'

'I don't just spend all day in bed,' she flared. 'I...I do other things as well.'

'Such as?'

'I wish you'd stop pretending to be interested in what I do and don't do.'

'And I wish you'd stop thinking that you can read me like a book. A trashy erotic novel with very big type.'

He gave her a crooked smile and she couldn't help herself. She smiled back. 'Now tell me what you do during the day.'

'I…well, actually, I'm taking a course at the moment.' Mattie lowered her eyes and wondered what had possessed her to divulge this personal piece of information.

She thought of Frankie, realised with an unpleasant little start that he had not crossed her mind all night.

'What kind of course?'

'Marketing,' she said abruptly.

'Marketing?'

'That's right! Marketing!' She glared at him and in her head she could hear Frankie's scathing criticisms of her desire to better herself, could hear him telling her over and over again that she just wasn't good enough to make the grade, that she had left school before getting any qualifications to speak of.

'Yes, I left school when I was sixteen! Yes, I'm not exactly what most people might see as ideal marketing material! But I can do this! Because I work nights in a nightclub and dress in skimpy little outfits doesn't mean that I don't have a perfectly good, functioning brain in my head! You might think that I'm a blonde bimbo but you're wrong!'

'I think it's a brilliant idea.'

'What…?'

'I said I think it's a brilliant idea.'

They looked at one another. Mattie's eyes drifted from his fathomless black ones down to his mouth, that sweetly sexy mouth of his, and she quickly looked away.

'Why did you leave school at sixteen?'

'I…everyone I knew was doing it…it seemed exciting at the time…getting out of school, becoming an adult, earning money…' She fiddled with the handle of the mug and stared down into the dregs of coffee at the bottom.

'And that was…how long ago?'

'Seven years.' Mattie dared him to share any caustic reflections on her academic non-achievements.

'And you never thought earlier about resuming your education?'

'It's not as easy as you make it sound!'

'Oh, where there's a will there's a way,' Dominic murmured. He watched the way her breasts rested lightly on the counter-top and hot blood surged through him. 'So, when does this marketing course finish?'

'I hand in my last project next week.'

'Then you quit the nightclub and get a job?'

'Then I hang on to my nightclub job because I still need the money and start the rounds of employment agencies. Sometimes the course supervisor can recommend someone for a job, but they have to be very good.' She stuck out her chin and remembered to scowl. 'So there's my potted life history. Not very exciting, is it? And now that we've had our little chat, I think it's time I made my way back.'

'Where does sleep figure in all of this?'

'I beg your pardon?'

'Sleep? You must be running on adrenaline and nervous energy. Let me make you another coffee.'

'I try and get at least six hours in the course of twenty-four.'

If Frankie allowed her. Usually, if he was in a particularly foul mood, he would think nothing of waking her up simply to commence an argument of sorts, even though he always backed off before he could push her to the absolute limit. Backed off and usually left the house.

'Here. Drink this. Then I'll drop you home. Or you could stay the night here. I have three bedrooms.'

'Stay the night?' Mattie looked at him incredulously. 'Are you completely mad?' She scrambled off the stool and reached for her jacket, which she had tossed on the counter.

Well, who could blame him?

The last thing she wanted to do was spend the night in this apartment, even if she locked herself in a spare bedroom and then stuck a chair under the door handle for safe measure! Just knowing that he was sleeping not far away would guarantee a restless night. Because...because...

Because he was dangerous, she thought. Things were dangerous between them. He was just too much of everything that was bad for a girl's health. And she had enjoyed talking to him too much for her own good.

She feverishly began walking towards the door and he sprang from his stool and followed her, overtook her, leaned against the door so that she was compelled to halt her frantic escape and look at him.

'Don't.'

'Don't what?' Dominic asked softly. And then he couldn't help himself. He reached and stroked some strands of hair away from her face and then left his hand there, tangled in her hair. It felt good. Better than good.

'Don't do what you're doing,' Mattie whispered unevenly, although she couldn't seem to find the strength to pull away from him.

'I'm not doing anything. Yet.'

She whimpered and made a half-hearted attempt to draw back, but the light pressure of his hand against the side of her head was clogging up her thought processes.

'I said I'd talk and I've talked.'

'Maybe it's not enough.'

'You promised...'

'Did I? I don't think so. I never make promises I know I won't be able to keep.'

His hand had moved to cup her face and one finger traced the outline of her trembling mouth.

'I want to see you again,' he told her huskily. 'And again. And again.'

'I've told you, there's no point.'

'You've told me that we come from different sides of the tracks and that you're not for sale because you happen to work in a nightclub. Well, I'm not interested in buying my women and I don't give a damn about what side of the tracks you do or don't come from.'

He moved around, just an easy, graceful shift of position, so that now she was leaning against the door and he was in front of her. Then he propped himself against the door with the flat of one hand, and with the other he began to do the unthinkable.

He began to trail his fingers along the circular rim of her jumper.

Mattie had her hands pressed against the door, wanting to run but longing to stay just where she was and let her body carry on responding the way it was doing right now.

It had been a long time.

Even before she and Frankie had ceased all form of physical contact, apart from the very occasional hug when they both found themselves helpless victims of nostalgia, regret and awareness of the chasm between them, Mattie had found it impossible to respond to him. His touch had left her cold, made her want to curl up into a ball and hide away. For a long time, she had put it down to sheer exhaustion at the hectic hours she kept and the demands on her time. Then she had seen it for what it was—she no longer enjoyed being with him and that had simply extended to all areas of her life.

'Please, Dominic…'

His name left her lips like a breathless caress. She should have called him *Mr Drecos*. That would have established some distance between them.

'Look, Mattie, I know you think I've pursued you for no better reason than to get you into bed…'

'And haven't you?'

'I want to enjoy you.'

'I told you…' Mattie could hardly recognise her own voice. It was shaky and husky, probably because she felt as if she was gasping for air.

'And you want to enjoy me too.' His kiss as he lowered his head was as light and as unthreatening as a feather brushing against her mouth, but it still managed to turn her legs to jelly. They matched her brain.

'Is it a crime to give in to mutual attraction?'

This time his kiss was a little less unthreatening and far, far more shockingly potent, because he was doing things with his tongue, invading her mouth, exploring her until she could barely support herself against the door.

'Well, is it?' he murmured unsteadily, drawing back from her so that she felt the absence of his touch like a sudden, yawning hole inside her.

'You're confusing me.'

'Good. I want to confuse you. Just as you confuse me. I want you to shiver every time I cross your thoughts and I want to send every nerve in your body into disarray whenever I touch you.'

He was virtually making love to her with his words, something she had never experienced in her life before.

But then, her only lover had been Frankie and words had never been his strong point. Looks, yes. The Irish blood in him had given him those all right, but that was as far as it went.

She was up against a different species here and she knew it. And, knowing it, she struggled to get her own thought processes into working order.

She could hardly dredge up Frankie's face under the onslaught of emotion flooding through her like a tidal wave!

His hand, that damned hand of his, slithered to caress her bare skin under the jumper. Just the flat, hard lines of her stomach, not venturing anywhere higher up, but it was sufficient to make her catch her breath. In surprise. And, she thought chaotically, pleasure. No, pleasure was too mediocre a word. *Excitement.*

'So...will you spend the night here? With me? In my bed?'

'No...please...' Mattie clung on to what coherent common sense was still in play. 'This is...is ridiculous...' The hand crept fractionally higher.

His own patience astounded him. He could feel her trembling under him, wanting him, but he was still having to rein in his impulse to lift her off her feet and sweep her into his bedroom like a primitive caveman taking possession of his woman.

His hand was only inches away from her breasts. Beautiful, well-shaped breasts that he wanted to touch and suck and worship.

'We have nothing in common...'

'I can think of something we have very much in common, actually...'

'Go and play your games with your own type...'

'I don't have a type. Only bores have types.'

'Well, go and play your games with…with someone else…!' The scattered conversation had done what it needed to do. Gave her room to breathe instead of just waving and drowning under her panting senses.

Gave her time to remember the man waiting for her back at the house and the impossibility of her situation.

She wriggled slightly and the hand that had been doing such dangerous things to her stomach found what it had been edging towards.

Mattie literally jumped as his long, expert fingers worked their way over her breast, found the nipple pointing and aching under the lacy bra and rubbed it.

One more minute and she could say goodbye to any kind of self-restraint.

'No!' She pushed his hand and he removed it immediately but only so that it could join his other hand, still lying palm down against the door.

He looked at her in the trap he had managed to create, with both his hands caging her in.

'We're both adults,' he said flatly, determined to knock through her defences, 'and we're both attracted to one another. And there's no point denying it.'

'All right, then! I won't deny it! But it still isn't going to happen!'

'Why the hell not?'

'Because I'm living with someone. Because I happen to have a boyfriend!'

CHAPTER FOUR

Now that her final project was done and dusted, Mattie had a sinking feeling that the hard work had only just begun.

That she would pass with flying colours, she had no doubt. She had been committed to the course from day one, had managed to hand almost all her work in on time, had been ahead of the rest for the past few months. But the course co-ordinator, a snappy-looking woman with a brisk attitude towards her students that bordered on the terrifying, had been blunt. Marketing was a competitive field and, marks or no marks, Mattie lacked experience. That she was brimming over with enthusiasm and talent unfortunately took second place to someone who had been working in the field for years. She would do her best but anything she came up with might involve disappointing pay and an ability to grapple with the bottom rung of the ladder without resentment.

The two employment agencies she had visited over the past week had more or less said the same thing but packaged a bit more attractively.

Mattie consoled herself with the thought that one week was not very long in terms of finding a job.

On another, less reasonable level, she was relying on the anxiety involved in a job hunt to keep her mind from swerving dangerously back to Dominic Drecos and the precipice she had almost succeeded in stepping off.

But at least she could relax a bit more now. No night-club tonight and no Frankie.

He had been peculiarly silent on the topic of her completed course but had compensated for the temporary break in hostilities by spending most of his time out of the house.

When she had questioned him two days previously on his whereabouts, he had responded in his typically aggressive manner.

Mattie kicked off her shoes, let the undisturbed peace of the house settle over her, contemplated switching on the television but wondered whether she really needed to be bombarded by a choice of desultory eight-thirty Sunday-evening viewing, and decided against it.

Easier just to slouch in the chair, eyes closed, and let her mind roam.

It was a little disturbing to find that it was roaming an awful lot more on Dominic Drecos than it was on Frankie, even though there were a million and one things she knew she needed to sort out with her boyfriend, things that could no longer wait for a convenient moment.

What was Dominic thinking of her?

She had walked out of his apartment, left with the snapshot image of his dark, stunned face at her revelation.

Her imagination had been more than willing to fill in the remaining details. The revulsion he would have felt for her, for thinking that she had responded to him, led him on perhaps, when she had not been in a position to lead anyone on. She would have lived down to his worst expectations, would have confirmed his thoughts that she was nothing but a waitress in a nightclub, huffing and puffing and playing hard to get when in fact her morals were of a decidedly shady nature.

Maybe he had even considered the possibility that her

behaviour had been nothing more than an act to try and hook him. The minute she started thinking along those lines, a whole host of other, nasty little thoughts sprang out from their dark corners and she was reaching for the remote control as a last-ditch effort at distraction, when she heard the peal of the doorbell.

Mattie hesitated. It took a few split-seconds to register that it couldn't possibly be Frankie because he had his own key, at which she caught herself heaving a sigh of relief and heading for the front door.

Her relief lasted precisely the precious few moments it took her to swing open the door and comprehend the fact that the person lounging against the doorframe in front of her was the last person she had expected to lay eyes on again. Ever.

'What are *you* doing here?' Antagonism laced her question but her heart had leapt treacherously inside her at the sight of him. This time in casual clothes and all the more impressive for it. Cream trousers, a cream shirt collar peeping out above the rugby-style jumper. The colours accentuated his swarthy colouring in a way his dark work clothes hadn't and she had to fight not to let any expression show in her eyes.

'I thought I'd drop by and size up the competition,' Dominic answered, getting to the point immediately and taking advantage of her momentary speechlessness to nudge his way through the door and into the house.

'You did *what*? Are you *mad*? And how did you find out where I live? No, let me guess, Harry told you!'

He had strolled towards the poky sitting room, glancing up the narrow staircase *en route*, and now proceeded to look around him with unabashed interest.

'Hm. Interesting method of colour co-ordination. Somehow I had associated you with a lot more flair.' He finally turned to look at her. How did she manage to look so damn good in a pair of baggy jogging bottoms and a T-shirt that went a long way to hiding every feminine curve of her body? 'So where is the boyfriend?'

His tone was light but his eyes weren't. She could read the message there and it sent a shiver down her spine. He had come to confront her over her duplicity because he was a man who would not walk away from a liar without first making his feelings known. Never mind that rubbish about coming by to check out the competition.

'Out. And his name is Frankie. You can't stay here. If Frankie came home now, he'd…'

'He'd…what?'

'Look, if you want me to apologise for…for not telling you sooner, then OK. I apologise. I should have told you from the very beginning.'

'So why didn't you?'

'Why didn't I *what*?' Mattie demanded. Even standing feet away from her, he still seemed to dominate the small room and drain her lungs of oxygen. And against him the room faded into ugly shabbiness that seemed to point accusingly in her direction. No wonder he had made that sniping little remark about being disappointed with the lack of flair.

'A cup of coffee would be nice. Black, no sugar.'

'You can't stay for a cup of coffee! You shouldn't even *be* here! Harry isn't going to get away with this! Giving my private address to any and everyone!'

'I'm not any and everyone,' Dominic contradicted coolly.

'OK! Well, anybody who flashes an impressive business card and makes vague promises about being able to help him financially at some point in the future! You know what I mean! You have to leave. Now. Frankie could get back at any minute…'

'I'm beginning to think that you're scared of this boyfriend of yours.' She certainly wasn't in love with him. Not if she had responded to *him* the way she had. He had spent the past week at the mercy of a thousand thoughts about her, angry with himself for being taken in, furious because he still couldn't seem to get her out of his head and finally harshly reasoning that he was completely justified in doing his utmost to seduce her, considering she had strung him along.

'Does he hit you?' Dominic asked without taking his eyes off her face.

'Don't be ridiculous! Of course he doesn't hit me! Do you think I would ever stay put with a man who raised his hand to me?'

'Then what are you doing with him, because you sure as hell don't love him?'

'And you just *know* that, do you? After a couple of conversations with me, you're suddenly qualified to make conclusions about my personal life, are you?'

The brooding intensity of his stare was shattering her composure as utterly as he had managed to shatter it a week ago when he had touched her.

He began walking towards her very slowly and Mattie backed away, then remembered that he was in her territory now, and uninvited, and stood her ground until he was standing right in front of her with his hands thrust into his trouser pockets.

'Got it in one. So tell me what you're doing here with a man you don't love when you'd much rather be with me.'

'You're an arrogant swine! You know that, don't you?'

'Yes, but I still like to hear you say it.' His expression didn't change but there was a sudden ironic humour in his voice that had the ground beneath her feet shifting once again.

She sighed dramatically and gave up.

'I'll make you your coffee and then you go. Deal?'

'No. But I accept the offer of the coffee anyway...'

He followed her back into the tiny hallway and out through it into the kitchen. Mattie could feel him just there behind her, a dark, overpowering presence that was sending her nervous system into fierce overdrive.

She had grown quite accustomed to the house. Now, though, she was seeing it through his eyes. He'd probably never been inside a place as small and unkempt as this one. A lifetime of wealth would have protected him from ever getting too close up and personal with this particular vision of reality.

And the kitchen wouldn't improve his ideas either.

At first, when she and Frankie had moved in, she had felt some enthusiasm to do something with the place. After all, it wasn't as though they were renting. The house had belonged to his parents, an ex-council house that had suffered from lack of essential home improvements. But life just seemed to get in the way of her good intentions. First there was Frankie, slumped in depression after his mother faded away in a hospital from lung cancer, leaving him the house and the memories but unfortunately no siblings with which to share the burden of her passing away. Then his own accident and his sharp spiral downwards. Not to mention her own time spent juggling jobs and study.

Who had time for stripping walls and plastering over cracks?

She held her head up high as she walked into the

kitchen, switching on the kettle and reaching for a couple of mugs before finally turning to look at him.

'I can see what you're thinking. There's no need to make it so obvious.' Mattie folded her arms protectively and tried to insinuate a bit of distance between them, which was nigh on impossible because of the dimensions of the room.

'What am I thinking?' Dominic perched against one of the counters and gave her a long, measured look.

'You're thinking what a dump I live in.' The kettle was boiling. She spun around and began making the coffee, but her hands were trembling.

'Why don't you move out?' Big question and, if she but knew it, she might have guessed that he wasn't just referring to the house but to the man she shared it with.

Thinking about him was enough to make Dominic clench his fists in jealousy. Primitive, green-eyed, monstrous jealousy. An emotion he had never succumbed to in his entire life and one which left him shaken and confused. As emotions went, confusion didn't do it for him.

'Take one guess, why don't you? Here's your coffee.' She moved to sit on one of the pine chairs at the small kitchen table. 'You can sit if you want.'

'The money? Is that why you stay here?'

'We don't pay rent for this. It was Frankie's parents'. His father died when he was twelve and his mother left it to him when she died a few years ago.'

Dominic sat down facing her. He wanted her to tell him everything, why she was here, why she had stayed here and not cleared off. What her relationship was with the boy. It sure as hell wasn't love because this house did not speak of love. No homely touches. No pictures of the two of them cluttering the surfaces. Nothing that seemed to have been bought with joint effort and affection.

Or so he told himself.

The alternative was that he had chased a woman who had a boyfriend, saw him as a nuisance and wanted him out of her life without further ado.

Pride fought against something else…whatever emotion it was that had driven him to come here tonight.

'When did you hand in your final paper?' he asked abruptly, surprising her with the change of subject, and Mattie allowed herself to relax a little bit.

'On Friday.'

'I'm surprised you're not out celebrating.'

'On a Sunday?' No celebration. She had gone out to work as usual. Come home to an empty house and Frankie had not returned home until lunchtime the following day.

'You never told me where the boyfriend is.'

'He's…he's out with some of his mates. At the local, I expect.' She looked away with a telltale flush.

'Spends a lot of time there, does he?'

Mattie was horrified to find that tears had sprung up behind her eyes, and she tightened her jaw in an attempt to bite them back. She wouldn't cry. She had stopped crying a long time ago and she wasn't going to let this man get to her like this.

'You don't understand.' She took a few deep breaths and managed to get control of herself once again. Enough for her to raise her eyes to his although the unexpected gentleness of his expression was almost her undoing. 'It's all right for you. You've never known what it's like to open your eyes and know that each day is going to be a struggle. Sometimes it's easy just to give up and take the simplest road to dealing with things, which is usually the road leading to the nearest pub.'

Dominic said nothing. He continued to nurse his mug and look at her.

'A lot of people face a life of struggle. Most people aren't born into privilege. But most of them don't become alcoholics in the process.'

'Frankie's not an alcoholic!'

'Why are you defending him? You work in a night-club because, you tell me, the money's good and you need the money. From which,' he carried on inexorably, 'I take it to mean that you need to pay the bills because he doesn't have a job.'

Mattie's green eyes were stormy with helpless anger but she couldn't reply. He was right, after all.

'He…he's going to get one.'

'In between his visits to the pub with his mates?' Dominic laughed harshly and saw her wince. 'Are you sure he's with his mates?'

'What do you mean?'

'You know exactly what I mean.'

They stared at one another in silence for a few tense seconds, and Mattie was the first to break it by rising to her feet and swinging around so that she wasn't looking at him. There was a stack of filthy dishes in the sink. She added her mug to them and began washing up, hoping that her hands weren't shaking so much that she would drop something.

'There's no one else.'

'You sure about that?'

'Why have you come here? To drag an apology out of me? You don't have to do that. I've already apologised.'

'It occurred to me that maybe you and your boyfriend

had plotted behind my back. The man who shares a pillow with a woman is a man who is inclined to be generous with his lover. Maybe you figured between yourselves that if you managed to get me into the sack then it would just be a question of time before you could begin the process of bleeding me for money.' He hadn't considered anything of the sort, but he had to fire her up to anger, had to get her to spill her fury onto him and, in the process, her feelings, because she had been eating away at him for the past week.

Mattie spun around as though she had been struck.

'That is the most…most…*horrendous* thing you've said to me yet! How dare you?'

She walked towards him with the tea cloth in one hand, glaring. And Dominic just wanted to yank her down onto his lap and kiss the expression off her face.

'I'm an extremely rich man. Wealth breeds suspicion.'

'Then I feel very sorry for you indeed!'

'It wouldn't be the first time that I've been pursued by a gold-digger.'

'If I *recall*, you were the one doing the pursuing!' She was standing directly in front of him now and leaning towards him in outrage at his suggestion.

'True. But maybe you're the clever opportunist who seized the chance when it presented itself…'

'You're…you're…'

'Someone accustomed to reading motives behind every action…'

'I'm not interested in your stupid money! And I would *never* hatch a plot like that with anyone!'

'Not even with the man you defend so eloquently, not even the man you live with and love?'

Dominic stared into the furious face that was pushed towards him.

'I don't *love* Frankie! I might live with him but I don't *love* him!'

He heard her swift intake of breath as her brain caught up with her admission and he couldn't help himself. He half smiled and then raised both his hands to tangle into her hair and frame her face.

'And I never believed for one moment that you were a gold-digger…'

'You tricked me.' Mattie pulled herself out of his grasp and realised that, rather than feeling angry at his verbal cleverness, she felt a certain reluctant admiration. The man had technique, that much had to be conceded. No wonder he was top of his tree.

She sat back down to look at him.

'So tell me why you're here.'

'Because…because I can't afford to be anywhere else. No. That's not why. At least, that's not the whole reason.' She threw him that wary, narrowed glance that he was getting used to, the one that crawled under his skin and made him have unholy thoughts of possessing her, peeling away that defensiveness like the outer skin of an onion to reveal all the complex layers underneath.

'Then what is? Tell me.'

Mattie looked down at her fingers resting lightly on the top of the table and then stole a glance at him.

'We sort of grew up together, then when we were teenagers we went out. Frankie was always the one the girls fancied. Good-looking, athletic…' She smiled to herself and Dominic felt a tight sensation of rage that even in retrospect this man could command a smile like that.

'He was going to be a footballer. That was all he'd ever wanted. He'd play for a team in the premier league, earn a fortune, fulfil his dream. Then when he was nineteen his mum died and he sort of collapsed.' She was still staring at her fingers and half talking to herself, but she could feel those dark, shrewd eyes on her face, watching her.

'By then, I was thinking of leaving him. I think I'd outgrown him. I still liked him but...' Now, that was something she had never really admitted, not even to herself, but talking was putting everything into perspective.

'But you wanted to get on with your own dreams?' Dominic inserted the question without disturbing the atmosphere, and he saw her nod slowly.

''Course, I couldn't then. Couldn't walk away from him when he needed my support, so I kind of postponed the course I'd applied for and carried on in my job. His mum and dad had bought this house from the council, oh, years ago. We moved in.' Mattie released one long, expressive sigh. 'I think I could do with a drink,' she said abruptly. 'Want one?'

Dominic shook his head and watched her open the fridge door, frown, pull out a can of lager.

'I don't normally drink this stuff,' she said, sitting back down and tugging the tab open. 'But...' She shrugged and swallowed a mouthful of lager straight from the can, watching him over the rim so that he wondered whether she was doing that just for his benefit. Another little ruse to elucidate that she was not the kind of woman who daintily sipped her lager from a chilled glass or, rather, that she was the kind of woman who drank lager at all.

He had to take his hat off to her. This woman was like none other he had ever met.

'You moved in...?' he prompted delicately.

'We moved in. For a while it worked. Then he went

out drinking one night and was involved in an accident. He was the passenger. Nothing serious, no one else involved...'

'What happened?'

'Car veered off the road and swung into a tree at the side. Trouble was...one of his legs was damaged.' She had only taken one mouthful, didn't really want any more than that. She had just needed the boost the touch of alcohol would afford her. Besides, she loathed drinking straight from the can. Now she cradled the cold can between her hands and looked at it.

'Not massively. But sufficient to ensure that he couldn't hope to become a professional footballer.'

'A tough blow.' He barely needed her to tell him what had followed, although she did, in the same low, thoughtful voice. The inevitable slide downhill, the anger, the frustration, the pity she had felt that had kept her tied to him.

'So, you see, I'm here for lots more reasons than simply the fact that I don't have to pay any rent.'

'You could transfer the money you spend on keeping him into paying for something of your own...'

'And how would Frankie cope?'

It was all Dominic could do not to shake her. 'Quite ably, I imagine,' he said instead, his voice silky, 'because he would have to. The need to survive without your help might go a long way to killing off the need to drown his self-pity in drink.'

Mattie stood up and he could see that her shutters were back in place. He was the millionaire and she was the streetwise kid. He had no doubt that she had come across boys from the other side of the tracks when she had been growing up. Had probably been targeted by one or two of them, with her amazing looks, and had developed a good line in switching off.

'I'll see you to the door, shall I?' She waited for him to stand up and then preceded him to the front door, where she waited patiently for him to finish his lazy stroll through the house.

'So there you have it. Now you can go away, safe in the knowledge that you weren't in any danger of being lured into parting with your precious millions by the likes of me.'

'By the likes of you…' Dominic murmured, leaning against the door and looking down at her. 'I can see why your boyfriend ended up taking refuge in the bottle…and whatever or whoever else he takes refuge in…but why the chip on *your* shoulder?'

'I don't have a chip on my shoulder.'

'Of course you do. A chip the size of a house.'

'Because I haven't leapt joyfully into bed with you?'

'Because you keep trying to make me see that the lines between us are inviolable.'

'They *are*.' Underneath the insistence in her voice she could also hear panic and she hoped that he couldn't as well.

'Well, your affair with this Frankie character you grew up with didn't work out, did it?'

The question, along with its obvious implications, hung in the air like an accusing finger. Mattie shrugged.

'He needs me.'

I need you too, was the first thought that rushed to Dominic's head and it left him shaken. *Need?* Need never entered his relationships with the opposite sex. Lust, yes. Want. Affection. But never need and certainly never love, as he had discovered to his own cost.

'You're his caretaker.'

'That's not true!'

'Of course it is. Clucking around him, overlooking his shortcomings and doing yourself out of a life in the process.'

The accusing finger was doing more than hover now. It was jabbing at her conscience like a knife.

'I am *not* doing myself out of a life! I've just completed my course!'

'For which, I presume, your beloved Frankie gave you all the unstinting help and support you wanted?' The answer to that one was written in the delicate blush that invaded her cheeks.

'He…he has his own personal demons to sort out,' Mattie mumbled, lowering her eyes so that she didn't have to meet the cool comprehension in his. She wished he would move from the door, so that she could pull it open and put an end to this hideous unravelling of her private thoughts, but he obviously was intent on staying put.

Until what? she wondered.

'And you're going to stay with him until he sorts them out?' Dominic enquired coolly. 'However long it takes? Make sure he's all right before you give yourself the opportunity to live your life the way you want to? You'd better pray that no further mishap befalls him or else you might find yourself growing old in the company of a man you've forgotten how to love. Pity is no basis for a relationship.'

Mattie looked up at him, ready for a fight. Fighting might take the edge out of the truth that he was forcing her to swallow, as though he had every right.

'Oh? And what *is*? If you're so clever when it comes to relationships, I'd love to know how come you're not in one.'

Touché, Dominic thought wryly. He looked at her standing there, and wondered what she would do if he reached out and enveloped her in his arms. Which was what he wanted. That and a great deal more.

'Is this a case of *I told you my life story, now you tell me yours*?'

'It's only fair, considering you've spent the past hour preaching to me on what I'm doing wrong in my personal life.'

'What's my incentive for telling you my life story?' Of course, he had no intention of doing any such thing, but the alternative was to walk out of the front door he was currently managing to barricade, and he had no intention of doing that either.

'Fair play?'

'Interesting concept.'

This wasn't the fight she had been hoping for. This was flirting and all the more dangerous because it was subtle. Every nerve-ending in her body was standing to attention. The aggressive *I-can-take-care-of-myself-thanks-very-much* girl she had been at pains to display had taken a distinct back seat to someone she didn't recognise, to a *kiss-me-senseless* creature that made her giddy.

'I don't confide in people as a rule.' Dominic crashed through her jittery thoughts and his mocking smile made her feel even hotter and more bothered than she was already feeling.

'No?' Mattie asked faintly.

'No. People have a nasty habit of storing up confidences and then using them against you at some future date.'

'There won't *be* any future date between us, so your secrets will be safe with me.'

'You need to tempt me just a little bit more.'

'Yes? And how would you suggest I do that?' Stupid question. He had led her with her eyes wide open straight into the little trap he had set. What he wanted her to do was obvious in the dark, slumberous expression in his eyes. And what was even worse was that it matched the hot thread of desire that was surging through her like a toxin.

'No way. I've told you, I'm not up—'

The sentence was unfinished as his mouth claimed hers and hell, it felt good. She was aware of her half-hearted attempt to push him away, just a formality, then with a muted groan she was returning his kiss with shocking enthusiasm.

Her hands wound upwards, around his neck, and then her fingers were in his hair, pressing him towards her as her mouth responded to his probing tongue.

Their positions altered, with Dominic shifting away from the door, his mouth never leaving hers as he propelled her against the wall by the door, captured her there with his mouth and his hands, which wanted to touch everything even though he knew the wisdom of reining in that particular instinct at this point in time.

He contented himself with just feeling her melt beneath him and hearing her soft little moans that were driving him crazy with desire.

When they finally drew apart, their expressions were equally ragged.

'Tell me that again,' Dominic demanded, but in a voice that could melt ice. He played with her hair, tucking some behind her ears, twirling strands around his finger.

'Tell you what?'

'That you're not up for…grabs? Was that what you were going to say?'

'You're no good for me,' Mattie murmured. 'I know you say that lines between people aren't inviolable and maybe they're not. But the way I feel, I would be the waitress to your tycoon and just feeling like that would make anything we had a farce.'

Dominic repressed the urge to thunder some sense into her. They wanted one another. The language of their bodies said it all. Wasn't that enough? he wanted to demand.

'You can't stay here,' he said instead. His voice was rough with suppressed emotion.

'I can't leave. Not yet.'

'And, in the meantime, I walk away from what we have…'

'We don't *have* anything.'

'What we *could* have, correction.'

'You've learned never to confide and I've learned never to speculate.' She was finally getting herself back into some semblance of control but his proximity was still suffocating her. She wriggled and he immediately stepped back.

His face was dark and scowling, and she couldn't stop herself from feeling just the slightest kick at the sight. Then the reality of her situation closed over her again. Frankie. No job. Waitressing in skimpy clothes to make ends meet. And this man who could take her in a minute, whose eyes made her burn, who was so totally unsuitable. In every respect.

'Go.'

'This isn't the end.'

Mattie gave another of her evasive shrugs. She opened her mouth to say something, anything, but never got there because they both heard the key in the door at precisely the same time, and as she turned around she could feel his eyes scan her averted face urgently.

What the heck had she been thinking? That Frankie would never reappear? Had she been so caught up with Dominic Drecos that she had managed to completely forget all about reality?

This is reality, she told herself fiercely, and don't you forget it.

Frankie staggered in, adopted the usual belligerent expression he assumed whenever he was drunk and confronted by her, then noticed Dominic standing to one side, very still, not in the least embarrassed. That changed his expression, Mattie noticed. From glowering to stupefied, all in the space of a couple of seconds.

'Who the hell is *he*?' His words were slurred but his brain was still operating.

Dominic moved forward, not bothering to extend his hand in any form of greeting. Nor did he bother to introduce himself by name.

'Your replacement,' was all he said. Mattie could barely look at him. *How could he?*

Then he was gone. No rush. Just one last contemptuous stare at an inebriated Frankie.

CHAPTER FIVE

'WHAT'S going on, Mats?' He looked bewildered and vulnerable and a wave of pity swelled inside her. She didn't know who she hated more, Dominic for bringing about this situation or herself for allowing it.

'We need to talk, Frankie. Tomorrow. When you're...'

'Not the worse for wear?' He laughed bitterly. 'Might as well get it over with, I say. This little talk of ours.' He managed to make it to the sitting room, where he promptly collapsed into a chair with his eyes closed.

Mattie wondered whether he had fallen asleep, but then he rubbed his eyes, opened them and looked at her.

'D'you have to stand there in the doorway like a bloody sergeant major?'

'Look, Frankie...' She took a few steps into the room then sat on another chair and pulled her legs up so that she was hugging her knees, giving herself the moral strength she needed when her insides were feeling like jelly.

'How long's it been going on, Mats? A month? Two months? A year?' He covered his face with his hands, but when he next looked at her there was no expected anger or jealousy in his eyes, just a kind of sad regret.

'Nothing's going on, Frankie. You have to believe me. I met him just over a week ago at the club. Well, he met me, actually. Followed me. But nothing happened between us.' She thought of the kisses that had ravaged her and made her want to drink up all of him. They might well have slept together because the infidelity had already been committed in her head.

'Don't blame you, Mats.' This time there was an edge of self-derision to his laughter that made her blood run cold. 'Look at me. Think I don't know what I've become? Not much of the man you thought I was going to be, eh, Mats? Bit of a loser, all told.'

'No.' She could feel tears prick the backs of her eyes and she went over to where he was slumped on the sofa and wrapped her arms around him, the way a parent might wrap her arms around a child who had been hurt. Except she couldn't kiss the hurt and make the pain go away.

'Me and you, we ain't going anywhere, Mats.'

'Don't say that, Frankie. I... You know how much I...'

'Loved me once? Yeah, I know all that.' He held her arms and ran his fingers along them. It was the first time they had had any physical contact for a very long time, and there was no charge behind this physical contact now. Just the affection born of years of knowing one another.

'I still love you, Frankie. I'd never hurt you, not in a million years! And Dominic is no one. We never made love.'

'And I never meant to hurt you, pet, but we bring each other down. No good us denying it. Once I was going to be somebody, then the accident and everything got lost. Me, you, us. Two kids playing at housekeeping, that's all we were.'

'Don't say that.' The errant tear turned into a silent stream.

'I know you haven't got anywhere to stay, Mats and

I'm not going to chuck you out. I'd never do that. You can stay here for as long as you want, but...'

She'd thought of all of that, had known the truth of every word he was saying now, but she felt like a piece of glass suddenly splintered into a thousand pieces. For good and bad, Frankie had always been her certainty, even though they were bad for one another.

'I've given you hell these past few months, Mattie. Hated myself for doing it but I just couldn't seem to help it. Don't cry, pet. Here, got a hankie somewhere. No, I haven't sorry. Use my shirt.'

'I shouldn't have done that course. I should have stayed where I was. You were right.'

'You're talking rot and you know it.' He sighed and wrapped his arms tighter around her. 'I was jealous, was all. Seeing you moving on like that, and me without a job, down the boozer all the time. Us not talking like we used to. Mats, we were kids when we met and then stuff happened and we grew up but...'

'No, don't say it,' Mattie whispered.

She knew what he was going to say. She had thought it herself over time, but she still wanted to shut the words out.

'We weren't meant for one another, Mats. Not really. Lord, we haven't even touched one another for months. Time was when we couldn't keep our hands off each other! Remember how it used to be? When we were young?'

'I can't walk away from you, Frankie. Not after everything we've been through.'

'You need to, Mats. Can't keep depending on your goodwill all my life, now, can I? Tomorrow I'm going to clear out for a while. You can have the place, move out when you're good and ready.'

'Where will you stay?' She raised her tear-streaked face to look dully at him.

'Never you mind that. I've got friends.'

The conversation rang in her ears for days afterwards. She carried it around inside her like an invisible weight.

Except it wasn't one.

Just the opposite. It was like a fog that had suddenly begun to clear, and maybe it was her growing optimism that she could grasp her life and take control of it that attracted the attention of Lady Luck.

Lady Luck in the form of a potential job, not through the employment agencies as she had expected, but through Harriet Newton, the formidable course co-ordinator, who called her in because, in her words, she had a pleasant surprise in store for her.

'Naturally, it's not a given,' she warned. 'But an interview is a vital step and you...' she looked critically but kindly at her most enthusiastic student '...should have no problem impressing any potential employer...'

And her luck just ran on and on until she had to pinch herself just to make sure that it all wasn't some delightful dream from which she would awaken and find herself back in her wretched, stalemate situation.

True to his word, Frankie got in touch only by phone, seemed a lot happier than he had been living with her, actually congratulated her on her job offer and sounded as if he meant it.

She almost expected him to come over so that they could discuss the business of her moving out, and when, ten days after she had been accepted by Devereux Group, she heard the peal of the doorbell she sprang to her feet, knowing that this conversation now would not be half as painful as the last one they had shared face to face.

She was momentarily shaken to find Dominic standing outside, as devastatingly handsome as she recalled. Then, oddly, she felt a calm acceptance that he had come. She had known, somewhere inside her, that he would, and had been waiting for him. How on earth was that possible?

'Well, do I get an invite in or shall we simply stare at one another for a few more minutes?'

That dark, velvety voice! The same one that had invaded her dreams every night, the same one she had had conversations with in her head, telling him about what she had been up to.

'Sorry.' She stepped aside and he brushed past her and into the small hallway, but instead of walking into the sitting room he remained where he was until she had closed the door.

'You look...different,' he murmured, looking at her. It felt like years since he had set eyes on her. In fact, he had had to restrain himself from coming over to see her, knowing that whatever had transpired between her and Frankie would still be too raw for her to tolerate the sight of him.

And he wasn't going to risk scaring her away. Not when he had made his mind up that he would have her, come hell or high water. And have her on his terms, with her compliance freely given rather than being dragged out of her because her body was temporarily not obeying her mind. He wanted her to yield to him without any barriers in place, with every ounce of her being.

He needed to wait.

'Different?' Mattie laughed a little nervously. 'I've had my hair trimmed.' Don't you like it? she wanted to ask. 'That long hair was fine for the nightclub but...well, actually I don't work there any more…my last night was a week ago…'

Dominic lowered his eyes for a fraction of a second, then he looked at her once more and smiled.

'I take it a lot has happened with you. Why don't you tell me everything over dinner?'

All the old misgivings reared up into place, but then they were replaced by something she hadn't felt before in his presence, a sense of self-worth. Stupid, since she was still the same old person, but true.

'Sure. Why not?' She glanced down at her jeans and jumper and then grinned. 'Fast food somewhere, or do I have to make myself a bit more presentable?'

'Fast food?'

'You know what I mean. Dodgy chicken wrapped up in batter, semi-cold chips, plastic cutlery, fluorescent lighting, queuing system…' He looked so appalled at the prospect of that that she had to smother the instinct to burst out laughing.

'Bottle of cold Chablis, halibut, skate, *pommes frites*…'

'Oh. Fish and chips, in other words.'

'But grown-up cutlery,' Dominic grinned. 'I know a very good seafood place. You do like seafood, don't you?'

'My favourite. I'll go and change. Why don't you go and wait in the sitting room? Frankie…'

He watched the shadow flit across her face and insanely wished that out of sight was a little bit more out of mind. Correction, a whole lot more out of mind.

'Frankie won't be bursting in…'

She dressed quickly and carefully. Nothing at all sexy, nothing to remind him of the girl she had been. Chic, or at least as chic as she had been able to afford on her limited budget. Black skirt snugly fitting but reaching to her knees, a silky pink vest top with a matching cardigan, fairly flat black shoes which she had bought in preparation for her job, sheer black tights because summer was giving way to autumn and there was a nip in the air that hadn't been noticeable a few weeks ago.

When she finally looked at her reflection in the mirror, there was an excited gleam in her eyes that made her hesitate for a few seconds.

Then she was walking into the sitting room, feeling like a teenager on her first date.

He hadn't sat down. He was standing by the window, half looking out, his hand in his jacket pocket, and he turned as soon as she walked in.

'Better?' Mattie asked nervously. Her! Nervous! 'Or should I wear my diamond tiara?'

'The tiara might be just a little too much,' Dominic told her gravely, but heavens, she looked edible. The shorter hair suited her, gave her a tailored beauty that was even more alluring.

'So,' he murmured as soon as they were in his car and heading out towards Chiswick, 'no more Frankie?'

'No more Frankie.'

'Pleased?' He wished he could watch her, see the expressions on her face so that he could gauge what was going through her mind, but he needed to concentrate on the road and she was far too much of a distraction for sensible driving.

'Yes and no.'

'What does that mean?' His hands tightened on the wheel but he kept his voice low and steady.

'Things weren't right between us. I mean, it's good that…that we've both reached the same conclusion, but…he was a big part of my life for such a long time that it takes some getting used to…' Mattie cleared her throat. 'He let me have the use of his house until I found somewhere of my own, and guess what…?'

'What?' A twinge of guilt made his jaw tighten but it only lasted a second.

'I've been offered a job and…' she paused to add drama to what she was about to say next '…part of the deal is that they've offered me an apartment! Can you believe it? I couldn't, to start with, but this company is spearheading a marketing campaign for a massive complex in south London. Apartments, health facilities, shops, the lot! And while they're involved in the marketing, there's a perk afforded to some of the employees of an apartment on site. I can't believe how it all happened at just the right time. Isn't it fantastic?'

'Fantastic.' Another twinge of guilt but he consoled himself with the thought that she would have got there anyway. She had the dedication or else how could she have persevered with her course against all odds? And she had the talent. Top of her course from the minute she had stepped foot in the classroom.

'You don't sound very pleased for me.' And for some reason, that was hurtful.

'I'm incredibly pleased for you,' Dominic said abruptly. 'How did Frankie react after I had gone?'

'Not as I'd expected, actually. You don't think I'm capable of doing this job, do you?'

'If you're capable of studying by day and working nights, then you're capable of becoming the next prime minister.'

'Yes, well, I'll think about that. Although I don't suppose my background would work in my favour.'

'What do you mean that he didn't react as you'd expected?'

'He wasn't jealous. Just sort of resigned, really. In fact, he was the one who dumped me.'

Which was better, Dominic thought. That way, she would never wonder what might have been, and he didn't want her wondering what might have been. He wanted her free, free for him.

The restaurant appeared in front of them without him even realising that they had arrived. It was quaintly old-fashioned on the outside, but as they walked in he heard her brief intake of breath as she absorbed the luxurious surroundings. A lot of glass, a lot of chrome, home of the beautiful people who felt more virtuous when they were eating fish as opposed to meat.

'Don't say it,' he warned, leaning towards her so that his breath was a warm whisper in her ear.

'Don't say what?'

'That this isn't the sort of place you're used to.'

'This isn't the sort of place I'm used to,' she informed him, dutifully. But no one would have guessed. Heads turned, but there was just curiosity there, the curiosity at seeing two good-looking people entering a restaurant, and Mattie felt as if she had somehow taken a step into the bright new future lying in front of her like a Christmas parcel waiting to be unwrapped.

And when she caught Dominic's eye she felt as though he had read her mind and was amused at the conclusions she was reaching. That the lines between people had only ever been in her head. Weird.

Then they were fussed over, shown to their table, handed menus that were like scrolls and required rolling down.

'Mmm. Scallop mousse!' Mattie feigned sophistication. 'Halibut, seared, with a drizzle of wild-mushroom compote! All my favourites!'

Dominic sat back and looked at her with amusement. He could have watched her forever.

And, under that languid gaze, Mattie felt suddenly and unexpectedly shy. Where had the tough, hostile woman gone? He certainly hadn't changed. He was still out of her league and she told herself firmly that it would be better all round if she remembered that.

'So,' he said lazily, 'halibut, seared, with the mushroom compote today. What tomorrow?'

'You must think I'm a little ridiculous. All this fuss just because I'm getting out there in the real world. Well, not *real*, but…'

'You're grabbing your opportunities. Nothing ridiculous about that.'

'I guess the women…you socialise with have never had that dilemma.' Mattie smiled and was relieved when his attention was diverted by the arrival of the waiter to take their orders.

'No,' Dominic said truthfully. 'Most of them are just content to squander their opportunities. Naturally, I meet women in the course of work, career women who have worked damned hard to make their way to the top, women who command respect at the highest level, but equally I meet those whose ambition in life is to meet and marry a rich man who can support their extensive shopping habit for the rest of their lives.'

'And which do you prefer?' Mattie asked curiously.

It was a question that was spared an answer as wine was brought to their table, the Chablis he had promised, and poured into glasses.

'I don't categorise the women I find attractive.'

'Well, that's a non-answer if ever I heard one,' Mattie said dismissively, and Dominic grinned. 'And don't forget we made a deal…'

'A deal?'

'That's right.' She finished her glass of wine and watched as he poured her another.

Mattie had never been much of a drinker. She could feel the first glass go pleasantly to her head, eating away at the nervousness she had felt earlier on.

'I gave you my potted life history when we last met. Or, should I say, when you last appeared uninvited at the house? And you promised to give me yours.'

Starters were brought to them, which she barely noticed because she was so busy concentrating on the man sitting opposite her.

Dominic caught her eye over a mouthful of smoked salmon and looked at her. 'I thought you'd already summed me up. Or so you insisted on telling me every time we met. I thought you knew my potted life history.'

'Where did you grow up?'

'Greece and England. Greece for the holidays, England for the schooling. I was boarded from the age of eleven.'

'What was it like?' School had been a nightmare for her. She had loved the work, had been good at it, but the necessity to bend to peer pressure had been acute and she could see, in retrospect, that she had wasted her education. Reading books and studying were things that had had to be done covertly. Not that her parents hadn't encouraged her, but she sailed past their lectures on the importance of a good education with the blithe disregard of someone who was the lynchpin of teenage social life. The prettiest girl with the cutest boyfriend.

Now she listened enviously as Dominic chatted about his own school experiences, making her laugh as he told her stories about the other pupils there. Even at that age, he had already learnt to take for granted the fact that he

would achieve at school, move on to university, reach
the highest echelons of professional life.

And she found herself telling him about her own
school days. The girls who had smoked behind the bi-
cycle shed. The boys who had drunk. The truancy. The
teenage pregnancy that had caused such a stir at the time.
No knives, no actual violence, the school really hadn't
been that rough, but a lot of giggling in the back at the
cool kids who made a point of slouching in their chairs
and making ridiculous remarks just to see how far they
could push a teacher.

Somewhere along the line, she realised with a little
start, they had managed to finish the first bottle of wine
and were now well into the second.

She hadn't felt as relaxed as this in a long time. She
ate her fish, told him that it was not really any better
than fish and chips from a certain place she knew in
Shepherd's Bush.

'And will I get to make that judgement myself?'
Dominic asked lazily.

'Oh, no!' Mattie laughed, looked at him from under
her lashes in a way that she knew was provocative. 'It'll
all go downhill if the posh set decide to descend on it.'
But there was no rancour in her voice, and when he
laughed she heard herself laughing along.

'I could dress down,' Dominic told her with exaggerated gravity. If a nuclear bomb had been detonated he
would have been unaware, because all he could see was
this exhilarating creature sitting in front of him, with her
mobile, animated face and her expressive, slender hands.

'Hah. I bet you've never dressed down in your life
before.'

'Jeans? Sloppy shirt? Running shoes? I could do that.'
He stroked his chin thoughtfully. ''Course, it would re-

quire a shopping trip…' He knew she would be amused, would laugh, and he wanted to hear her laughter.

He signalled for the bill, still keeping his dark eyes firmly fixed on her face.

Mattie regretfully thought that the evening was over. 'I could get a taxi back to my place,' she said as he signed a credit-card slip. 'You don't have to drop me back.'

Dominic looked up at her and their eyes met with an understanding that sent a charge of electricity running through her.

'This has a *déjà vu* ring about it,' he murmured, standing up and waiting as she followed suit.

'We can't…' No use pretending that she couldn't read the intention in his eyes. Or, for that matter, understand the answering response it aroused in her. But alarm bells were ringing in her head. Bad enough enjoying his company because that was only one dangerous step away from becoming addicted to it. But to sleep with him…

'Why can't we?' Dominic murmured.

She felt the gentle pressure of his hand on her elbow as he escorted her to the door and had to clutch the wildly scattering strands of her common sense with an excited, frightening, hot feeling of being sucked under.

'Frankie and I have just finished with one another,' she said, pleading to herself and to him as well. 'I'm not on the market for another relationship.'

'Why should we fight what we feel? I'm going to call a taxi for both of us. I'm over the limit.'

'What about your car?'

'It'll wait here. I'll send my driver to collect it.'

'Which is why we can't become involved with one another!'

'Because I have to leave my car here overnight?'

'You're deliberately misreading me!'

'And you're deliberately trying to find excuses. Why?' He bent towards her so that she could breathe him in, that clean, masculine scent that made her suck her breath in sharply. 'Why are you so scared?' There was dark amusement in his murmured question.

'I don't want involvement,' Mattie protested weakly. Now the taxi was slowing down for them.

'What sort of involvement are you talking about? A man hanging around your neck like a dead weight? Having your freedom of movement restricted? Or, worse, dictated to? You had that with him, or have you forgotten? Believe me, I'm not looking for involvement either.'

The taxi stopped and Dominic's head dipped for him to give the cab driver his address, then he looked at her and shot her a slow smile that made the insides of her stomach curl.

'"To be or not to be…?"'

Mattie shuffled into the seat, sliding along to accommodate him. Hot, slick excitement was pulsing in her veins. She didn't quite know why she was arguing. For every argument she raised, he countered it with a response that was utterly reasonable.

'Do you prefer the safety of living with a man you pity and shutting yourself off from all other experiences? Habit can be a destructive thing, Mattie. In your case, the habit of being put down, stepped on, having your wings clipped.'

'Frankie didn't…' Oh, but yes, he had. He had wallowed in his own misfortune and used her pity as a battering ram against her. He had exhausted her, laughed at her aspirations and watched her slave to make money to grab a career for herself while he drank away whatever earnings that he could, without bothering to rouse himself enough to go and look for a job. He had been selfish, although his selfishness had had the same quality as a child's selfishness. That was probably why she had been able to handle it.

Dominic, however...

Mattie glanced sideways at him, met his eyes and shivered.

Dominic Drecos was no child. He was all, one hundred per cent man. He could hurt her in a different way. She knew that at some instinctual level, but at that same level she knew that he was an irresistible force.

'Stop finding excuses for the man,' he now said impatiently. 'You may have gone back a long time with him, but that didn't stop him from being a noose around your neck.'

'You're so cold and calculating,' she murmured.

'I'm realistic. We're both adults and we're attracted to one another. More to the point, neither of us is looking for commitment and marriage. Are we?'

'I definitely am not,' she said fiercely. 'You needn't fear that you might become tangled up with a woman who's totally unsuitable for you.'

'Is that what you think?' It was taking all his massive self-control not to reach out and touch her. He couldn't remember ever wanting a woman as much as he wanted her, or being forced to control himself the way she did.

'That there would be no chance of wanting a serious relationship with you because your background isn't the same as mine?'

Mattie gave a cynical little toss of her head. 'Not,' she said, 'that it makes any difference to me. Just trying to clarify the situation.'

'You mean you wouldn't be hurt if you thought that that was the case?'

The minute he said that, homed in with his usual accuracy on that vulnerable side of her that she had grown so accustomed to keeping under wraps, Mattie's hackles rose in immediate self-defence.

'Why should I be?' She shrugged. 'I've been pointing out our differences from the first moment we met. Just call it satisfying my curiosity.'

'And, as I've told you every time you've begun with your tired old arguments about us coming from the opposite sides of the tracks, your background makes no difference to me.' He gave an impatient shake of his head. 'Maybe it's because I'm not English so I haven't been inculcated with all that rubbish about social class. No, I don't want involvement because...'

'Because what?'

He looked at her in silence for a few fleeting seconds and then raked his fingers restlessly through his hair.

'Potted history, please,' Mattie told him. 'You're very good at dodging questions you don't want to answer and I'm tired of it.'

'You're...*what*...?'

'Well, you can't blame a girl for wanting to know just a bit about the man who wants to get her into bed.'

Dominic laughed and looked at her appreciatively. 'I'm beginning to think you put on that *me-working-class-girl* act just to get your own way. Am I right?'

'Bad relationship?' Mattie pressed. 'Some poor woman got a little too involved and became the proverbial noose around your neck, which is what you accused Frankie of being?'

'You turn me on.'

'You're changing the subject.' But those four words made her breasts ache and her body go to liquid.

Dominic looked at her thoughtfully, shifted a bit so that he was leaning against the side of the car, looking directly at her. If there was one thing this woman wasn't it was coy, and he was discovering, to his amusement, that he liked that.

'Six months ago I broke up with a woman called Rosalind.' *And you are the first person I'm talking to about this,* he could have added, but didn't. 'We had been going out for nearly a year and over that year she changed from an easy-going, enjoyable companion into a clingy, possessive woman who wanted to know my every move.'

'Which must have been a serious blow to a free spirit like yourself,' Mattie said drily, and in the darkness of the car Dominic flushed darkly at the well-honed dart.

'Do I detect a note of sarcasm in your voice?'

'If the cap fits… So then what happened?'

'Do I have to go into the details?'

'Yep.' She was enjoying this. 'What's good for the goose and so on and so forth.'

'Spare me the proverbs.' He leaned forward, resting his elbows on his knees, and wondered, not for the first time, why he was so taken with a woman who seemed to see a hurdle and automatically assumed it was there to be demolished.

'Spare me the evasion.'

'Well, if you must know, she began making calls to the office. Not just one call a day, or two, but literally dozens. In the end, I had to instruct my personal secretary to block them. When I tried to speak to her about it, she would cry. That famous fallback that women use with such alacrity when it suits them.'

'Excuse me. The women *you* know.'

'And you've never shed a tear?'

'Not as a form of emotional blackmail,' Mattie said with distaste.

'Well, she did. Later on, there was worse. Later on, she moved from tears to anger. Didn't I want to be with her? Eventually, I told her that it was finished, at which point she began stalking me. I would get home in the evenings to find her car parked outside, where she would be waiting for me to get home. It was a nightmare.'

Mattie reflected on this in shocked, subdued silence. 'What did you do?'

'I confronted her, told her that if she didn't stop I would be forced to go to the police, that her parents would get to know about it. Thankfully that worked, but that's why I'm, let's just say, a little cautious about further involvement with the fairer sex. So you see, our potted life stories have more in common than you think.'

They had reached his apartment block without Mattie really even realising they had been travelling. She got out, waited for him to join her, and then said, thoughtfully, on their way in, 'And how did you feel, you know, about…?'

'How did I *feel*?' This time there was no awkward sitting in the lobby. He was leading her straight towards the elevator, although, ludicrously, he still didn't know whether they would end up in his king-sized bed together. It frustrated the hell out of him.

'Yes, *feel*,' she was saying now. 'Were you in love with her?'

'I was very fond of her in the beginning.'

'What about love?'

'What about it?' The elevator doors slid shut. The mirrored sides reflected them. He could see those forthright green eyes watching him from every angle. And, in her head, Mattie was already climbing down from pushing him for an answer to that one, because she realised she didn't want to have an answer. She didn't want to imagine him hurting because he had fallen in love with a woman who had turned out to be the wrong woman for him. She preferred to stick with the option that he had been fond of her because…because…

She sighed with relief when the doors opened, but relief was short-lived, soon replaced with the steady beat of her heart, racing faster as he slipped his key into the door and pushed it open.

'History, Mattie,' he murmured, standing aside to let her brush past him. 'This is the present. For both of us, wouldn't you say…?'

CHAPTER SIX

HE MADE such perfect sense. Two people, disillusioned from their past relationships, helplessly drawn towards each other, both knowing the undesirability of becoming too involved.

Once bitten, twice shy, Mattie thought now. She seemed to be thinking in proverbs.

From all accounts, she and Frankie should have made the ideal match. They had gone from childhood friends to childhood sweethearts. They should logically have ended up as blissfully happy adults with the statutory two children and pet dog. Instead, it had all unravelled like a ball of wool.

And Dominic hadn't needed to tell her what she had assumed for herself. That Rosalind had breathed the same privileged air that he did, and that, despite that, the relationship had collapsed under the weight of its own inadequacies.

So here they were now, not looking for anything beyond the present.

And heavens, how she wanted him, wanted him with every fibre in her body.

She refused his offer of a drink, met his eyes steadily and felt shaken but delirious at the molten heat of his gaze.

'No drink for Dutch courage?' he asked, moving towards her, then at last giving in to his need to touch her, but only delicately, only capturing her face between his big hands so that he could stroke the sides of her cheeks with his thumbs.

'I only need Dutch courage if I'm about to do something I don't want to do,' Mattie said. She placed the flat of her hands on his chest and then began to unbutton his shirt with trembling fingers. Each undone button gave her a glimpse of his hard, bronzed torso and the muscular strength of his shoulders.

'You'd better stop that,' Dominic told her roughly, 'or you might find that we don't make it to the bedroom.'

He scooped her up and carried her towards one of the rooms, kicking open the door with his foot.

He made his way to his bed and deposited her gently, then proceeded to look at her for a few heart-stopping seconds, before switching on one of the lamps on the low chest of drawers that covered almost the length of one of the walls.

Then he returned to where he had been standing. That look. Mattie wanted to stretch like a cat and bask in the heat of it. She squirmed a little, sighed and then watched in fascination as he began undressing.

Anyone would think that she was a virgin witnessing her first glimpse of the male body in all its glory. Not that many were as glorious as his. If any at all.

He tugged off his shirt, exposing broad shoulders, a firm, hard stomach, flat brown nipples and then, as he slowly unbuckled his belt, Mattie's gaze drifted to where he was now unzipping his trousers and sliding them down over his lean hips.

'You do know,' he said with a low laugh, 'that when I'm done, it's going to be your turn…'

'I may have worn tight outfits when I worked at the club, but performing a striptease is not my kind of thing.' Her mouth felt dry as she watched him slip his fingers beneath the elasticated waistband of his boxer shorts and then a smile of pure, wicked satisfaction curved her lips at the sight of his impressive manhood.

'Well, we'll have to work on that, won't we?' He bent over her and began undressing her, savouring every second of his gradual exposure of her body.

Her skin was as smooth as satin. First her shoulders, then the rest of her with only her lacy bra modestly covering her breasts. A clasp at the front and it was undone. Dominic pulled aside both halves of the bra and groaned as he saw the generous pale mounds spill out, saw the rosebud circles that he had imagined caressing.

Mattie lay perfectly still, watching him watching her, and felt a swell of desire so powerful that she half closed her eyes and sighed under the force of it.

She wanted him to touch her. Her breasts were positively aching to be touched.

Instead he finished what he had started doing, removing the rest of her clothing until she was completely naked.

'Happy?' he asked unevenly. He covered her body with his and just looked at her for a few moments. More than anything, he wanted her to be happy, to know that she was coming to him with every part of her soul open and willing, no doubts, no shadows.

'Happy,' Mattie agreed, in a similarly unsteady voice. She reached up to coil her hands behind his head, and brought him down to kiss her. The kiss seemed to go on forever, slow, tantalising. The exploratory, leisurely kiss of two people for whom time had finally stood still.

'I feel like a teenager,' she finally laughed breathlessly, and he smiled at her.

'We should have met when you were.'

'Oh, at sixteen I was besotted with Frankie.' Mattie

reached up to deliver a series of fluttery kisses on his mouth, moving her body sinuously beneath him and loving the feel of his hardness pressing against her.

'Because you hadn't yet met me.' He moved down, trailing his tongue against her collarbone and along the cleft between her breasts. Mattie held her breath, arched back and then released a long groan of utter pleasure as his mouth finally circled one nipple and he began sucking on it, tugging the tight bud into his mouth, grazing it with his tongue.

He captured her restless hands with his, splaying them out to either side while he continued to play with her breasts and tease them with his mouth. First one, then the other until her nipples were throbbing from the onslaught.

When she cried out, it seemed to be someone else's voice, coming from some other place.

This languorous seduction was like nothing she had ever experienced before. She knew that she was writhing beneath him, wanting more and wanting it now.

Although he was taking his time.

He had waited for this woman. Touching her, feeling her move, hearing her whimper for him—it felt as though he had been waiting for her all his life. He wasn't going to rush things now, even though if she so much as reached out and touched him he felt that he might have a struggle not to come. He was no long the master of lovemaking. The lovemaking was controlling him.

He released her hands and moved lower, feeling the taut flesh of her stomach with his mouth, then the indentation of her belly button, knowing that her body was responding instinctively now, her legs parting to accommodate his mouth.

Mattie gasped as his hands gently rested against the

soft inside of her thighs, allowing him unfettered access to the honeyed moistness of her femininity.

Then his tongue was playing games with that small bud, flicking across it until she wanted to scream with the exquisite agony that wanted release. Every so often, when he had taken her to the brink, he pulled back, waited for sensation to subside before starting again, tasting her, licking her, sending her to another planet, one she had never visited before.

Was it because he had had to wait for her to come to him that he felt so wildly and uncontrollably turned on? Dominic had no idea. Just looking at her, lying supine on the bed in all her glorious nakedness, had given him such a powerful charge that he had been momentarily bereft of thought.

And now, tasting her, feeling her move under him…

He eased his long body up and swivelled her so that she was lying on top of him. Her breasts dangled provocatively by his face and he captured one nipple in his mouth and sucked hard even as she sank neatly onto him, a tight, warm fit, moving with a perfect rhythm that matched his.

Their bodies were attuned to one another. United, as one, and when they finally soared upwards they soared there together in a shuddering orgasm that left him shaking.

Mattie collapsed onto him with a little sigh and eventually rolled off so that they were lying next to one another, then she turned to her side and propped herself up on one elbow so that she could look at him.

She could have feasted her eyes on him forever. Then she reminded herself that never was not a word that existed in her vocabulary, at least not when it came to him.

Nor was it one she would give house room to. Young she might be, but stupid she most certainly wasn't.

Dominic turned so that they were looking at one another, and he gently pushed her hair back, then pulled her onto him, tucking her head just under his chin so that he could kiss her fine blonde hair.

'I suppose I should be thinking of heading back home,' Mattie eventually said. She made a few circles on his chest with her finger, then delightedly traced the outline of his nipple.

'Why?'

'Because it's usually where I spend the night?'

'Usually?'

'Well, always.'

'There's no need for you to go back there,' Dominic told her, and Mattie laughed.

'What, you mean ever?'

She was teasing, he knew that, but even so the throwaway remark provoked a thought that flashed across his mind like a shadow, leaving as quickly as it had come, too quickly for him to reach out and take hold of it to analyse.

Dominic frowned slightly. 'I mean…'

'Don't worry, Dominic. I know what you mean.' Mattie's voice was dry but the reply was very quick and very unequivocal. She attempted to sit up and he tightened his grip so that she snuggled back down against him.

'Frankie's not there. All that's waiting for you is an empty house. Why go back there tonight? You can stay here, share my bed with me.' His voice was husky. 'I may be an old man but my stamina would surprise you.'

'You're not an old man. How old are you anyway?'

Old enough to be cynical, Dominic thought. 'Thirty-four.'

'Ten years older than me,' Mattie said lazily. 'The...' The perfect age gap, she nearly said, and then caught herself in time. Now, that would have been a dangerous observation, and she couldn't figure out why she would have made it anyway. 'The age when most men are married off,' she amended. 'Aren't your parents frantic for you to be settled and having a few grandchildren for them to coo over?'

'Frantic is a strong word. These aren't the Dark Ages any more.' His voice was laced with amusement. 'Keen, might be a better adjective. I'm an only child. My father would like to see something being done about the blood-line continuing and my mother thinks that I need a woman to anchor me. From my past experiences, I can say with my hand on my heart that anchoring is the last thing a woman has managed to achieve for me.'

Hence the perfection of their situation, Mattie thought. He had laid his cards on the table with her and now he could relax, safe in the knowledge that she wasn't going to pursue what was unattainable.

Which left her feeling just a little depressed.

'How is it that you didn't marry that boyfriend of yours?' Dominic asked. When he looked down, he could see the smooth line of her thigh curving across his and the push of her soft breast against his chest. He felt a moment of complete and pleasurable peace.

'Oh, just never got around to it,' Mattie said airily. 'These aren't the Dark Ages, you know.' She threw his cliché back at him and felt the rumble of his laughter under her. It was a good feeling. Too damned good. 'We ended up living together but then things weren't right between us. It would have been wrong to marry. My parents weren't overjoyed at us living together, of course, but they didn't press the issue.'

'Perhaps they knew that he was wrong for you and were happy to wait for you to come to your senses.'

'I'd never thought of that before,' Mattie said slowly then she shrugged. All this talk of marriage made her feel as if she was somehow, without realising it, standing on quicksand. In a minute, she could start sinking. 'Anyway, I really must go.' She pushed herself up and laughed when she saw the startled expression on his face, quickly followed by irritation.

'You still haven't explained why.'

'And I don't have to.' She stood up and looked around her, then spotted her clothes, which she began walking towards.

From his position on the bed, Dominic followed her progress and tried to stifle his massive frustration at her leaving. Shouldn't it be the other way around? he thought, scowling. Shouldn't the man be edging the woman away instead of the woman striding towards her clothes as if speed was now of the essence?

'I'll drive you back,' he grated, pushing back the rumpled bedclothes. 'And before you launch into a speech about being perfectly capable of getting a taxi back to your house, forget it. I'm dropping you home and seeing you safely to your door.'

Mattie paused and smiled sweetly. 'A lift back would be much appreciated.'

'Quite unnecessary,' Dominic continued to grumble, as they took the lift down and then walked out into the night air towards his car. He slung his arm around her shoulders and she linked her fingers through his. 'What's the point of having freedom if you don't utilise it?'

'By which you mean, accommodate you whenever

necessary?' She disentangled herself so that she could slip into the passenger seat of his car, and buckled herself in.

'Accommodate *both* of us, actually.' Instead of switching on the engine, he shoved the key into the ignition and proceeded to look at her, resting his head against the glass window of the door.

He could reach over right now and make love to her all over again. Right now, right here, like a sweaty adolescent without the privacy of a bedroom to fall back on. She turned him on. Not just her body, or the way she was looking at him now, eyes slightly contemplative, as if she was sizing him up but was not about to give him her verdict.

No, it was the way she was. Forthright, funny, private, with a mind that was as sharp as any he had ever encountered.

'Oh, really?' Mattie grinned. 'So you're thinking of both of us! Well, maybe another time. Now, perhaps we should get going? I expect you have a busy day tomorrow. Wouldn't want to be the cause of your not being able to function at work because you went to bed too late. Empire builders need their beauty sleep, I expect.'

'Witch,' Dominic muttered, but he started the engine and edged out of his parking slot. He would quite happily have taken a day off work if the plus side was spending all of it in bed with her. 'Just to fill you in, I can get by on very little sleep. I frequently do. As you must have when you were doing that ridiculous job of yours.'

'That *ridiculous* job was very handy when it came to paying bills,' Mattie said coolly, so that he was grittily aware that he had said the wrong thing. 'Some people do actually have to do *ridiculous* jobs simply to cover the cost of living.'

'Point taken,' Dominic muttered grudgingly. 'Not that I want to waste time on an argument about it.' He flashed her a sideways warning glance and Mattie relented. 'What are your plans for tomorrow?'

'Tomorrow?' She directed her gaze out of the window and frowned. 'I need to get some decent clothes for my job and then I shall try and see Frankie so that he can move back under his own roof. I have no idea where he's been staying but I'd bet on a floor somewhere.' Her voice softened. 'He's been brilliant over all of this. No recriminations, no post-mortems.'

Dominic's hands tightened on the steering wheel. 'What a hero,' he muttered sarcastically and she directed her frown to him.

If her head wasn't screwed on very tightly indeed, she might have been tempted to think that there was jealousy beneath that barely audible comment.

However, the thought of Dominic being jealous was almost laughable, especially when the jealousy pertained to her, a woman with whom he was having a thoroughly adult, uncluttered affair, if it even fell into that category.

No, a lot more likely was the fact that, being the man he was, he would on principle disapprove of someone like Frankie. Someone who had allowed himself to become a victim of circumstance and had reacted by drinking and shying away from looking for a job.

Mattie's lips tightened. 'I happen to think that it's quite heroic for him to let me have the use of his house when we're no longer an item. Would *you* have done the same in that situation?'

'That's hypothetical and I don't deal in hypotheses.'

'Huh. Sounds as if you lack imagination, in that case.'

But she couldn't find it in herself to have an argument with him. Their eyes met for a fleeting second and Mattie felt a shiver of such mutual compatibility that it frightened her.

'Something I've never been accused of before,' Dominic drawled.

Which made her think that perhaps he was referring to his imagination when it came to between the sheets, and she didn't want to think of him between the sheets with another woman. So she shrugged and said airily,

'Well, if you go out with paper dolls...'

He laughed, reached out to place the flat of his hand on her thigh, and her body started into immediate response.

'That's an unsafe driving practice,' she said a little breathlessly.

'Shame.' He removed his hand, leaving her leg feeling cold and deprived. 'We could always remedy the situation when we get to your house...?'

Mattie felt torn between her longing to fall in with him and her gut knowledge that she shouldn't. That she had to protect herself and that included laying down her own boundaries, so she shook her head very firmly.

'Then when am I next going to see you?' They had reached her house and he parked directly outside and killed the engine. 'If you're busy tomorrow, then I'll pick you up at seven-thirty on Friday. We could go somewhere for dinner.'

Mattie pushed open her door, expecting him to walk her to the front door, which he did. Though he couldn't possibly go inside. Not when she seemed so prone to losing control the minute she got too close to him.

'I'm not sure,' she said vaguely.

Not sure? What the hell did *that* mean? He swung

round in front of her and leaned against the front door, arms folded. He, of all people! The one man who abhorred possessiveness in another person! Who himself had never shown a sign of any such inconvenient emotion in his life before! Now finding himself in thrall to wanting to know every single thing she was planning to do that would exclude him from seeing her.

'I start work next Monday,' Mattie said. 'Do you mind moving? I can't get in if you're standing there.'

'Yes. You start work next Monday... So far, I'm following you. What I can't see is what that has to do with when I next see you.' Self-control, he told himself. He was a master of it. Or so he had always assumed. He wasn't feeling all that controlled at the moment, least of all with her looking up at him, keys in one hand, expression politely informing him that she wanted to get past him. He remained solidly in place.

'There's a lot to sort out before then. Frankie will want to move back here as soon as he can. I'm sure of that. Which means I shall have to move into the apartment some time over the weekend. I'm going to see the personnel manager on Friday morning to sort out the details and sign whatever contracts need signing, but, as the apartment was vacant, she did imply that I could move in at my own speed, and really I'd rather not stay here with Frankie if I can help it.'

Oh, no. No chance of that, Dominic thought with another unpleasant stab of possessiveness. Not if he had any say in the matter. He would be inclined to heave her kicking and screaming back to his own apartment if the alternative was sharing the house with her ex.

'You said that the apartment is...? Where exactly...?'

Mattie raised her eyebrows and gave him the address.

'Right.' He pushed himself away from the door and

looked at her with a hint of a scowl. Then he sighed and raked his fingers through his hair. 'You might need a hand with the moving... I can get hold of any size transport vehicle you might need.'

This time Mattie laughed out loud. 'Somehow I don't think that'll be necessary. My belongings can fit in the back of a sports car.' She reached out and found that she was stroking the side of his face, and before she could retract the mad impulse he took her hand in his, turned it over and kissed her palm, then he leant down and transferred his lips to hers.

Why on earth did he make her feel so...so *happy*? He looked at her and she shivered, he touched her and her whole body melted.

Was it because she had spent so long in a non-functioning relationship with Frankie that she was greedily lapping up this small bit of attention now, as though she had spent a lifetime starved of affection?

'Saturday,' Dominic murmured, breaking away from her but still leaning into her so that she could feel his warm breath on her face. 'Nine sharp. I'll be here to help you move.'

'Don't be ridiculous. I'm fully—'

'Yes, I know, *fully capable of doing it myself.* Why don't you just accept a little help for once, when it's offered in the best possible spirit?'

Except, what *was* the best possible spirit?

Of course, she should have stuck to her guns and calmly refused his offer to help her move. He would end up being an impediment, she was sure of it. But she didn't. And he showed up on the Saturday morning at precisely the time he had said he was going to. In a low-slung silver Ferrari that suited him down to a T.

Mattie watched as he got out of the car and snapped

her mouth shut because a woman with a mouth hanging open was not exactly an attractive sight. And besides, she was not impressed by cars.

Which she was very tempted to tell him as soon as she pulled open the front door.

'I'm here,' he said, grinning, 'and I've dressed down for the occasion.'

Mattie felt the corners of her mouth twitch as she took in his faded jeans, trainers and dark green sweatshirt. Then she nodded approvingly, thinking that he gave faded jeans a whole new meaning.

'And I've brought the statutory sports car.' He leaned against the doorframe and deposited a very chaste kiss on the tip of her nose.

'What on earth gave you the idea that all my stuff could fit into the back of a *sports car*?' Mattie laughed, spun around and waved her arms to encompass the pile of things patiently sitting at the bottom of the staircase.

Dominic strolled in and surveyed the collection with an expression of lazy amusement. 'Just as well I didn't listen to a certain woman who tried to say that she'd be travelling light, then, isn't it? My driver's parking outside now in a much more sensible Range Rover. We can follow him in the Ferrari.'

End of subject. Mattie hesitated and then sighed at her own unease. What was there to feel uneasy about? He had been right about her having to learn to accept help instead of always rushing up the steepest hill because of her pride. And it was a huge help having him there to help her move. Frankie had offered, but for some reason she had felt it important not to accept his offer. On some basic level, moving out of his house and into her own apartment, on loan though it might be, was the start of a new life for her. She would, of course, invite Frankie round in due course, but when the dust of their broken relationship had settled and their friendship could perhaps be resumed on a more casual basis.

He hadn't pressed the issue. In fact, he had looked a little relieved and had muttered something about having to get his own things together.

Which would have left her trekking across London on her own with all her bags in tow, more than she had expected.

Dominic's help was a blessing not to be scorned.

She smiled. 'Sure.'

'You go sit in the car. George and I will transfer the things to the back of the Range Rover. Anything you want to carry with you?'

'No. Just my backpack.' She looked at him, turned away as he sized up everything that needed to be transported to the apartment, and tried to stifle a very unliberated sense of pleasure at having the situation taken out of her hands. Being taken care of made a heady change from having to take care of someone else all the time.

She obediently went to the Ferrari and watched as Dominic and his driver ferried her belongings into the back of the four-wheel drive. Then the slow drive across a traffic-laden central London towards the block of apartments.

The development was going to be the biggest of its kind and proudly advertised the advantages of living south of the river. It encompassed private suites, which were currently in the process of being fitted to the highest possible specifications, offices, a floor entirely devoted to a state-of-the-art gym and various beauty rooms, conference facilities, underground parking, even an in-house cinema for the exclusive use of the residents.

All built around an open central area of grass, trees and a sprinkling of benches for whoever wanted to avail themselves of fine weather during the warmer months.

Mattie described it all in detail, only trailing off when she realised that she had been conducting a one-way conversation.

'You didn't have to come and do this,' she said, feeling her pride slip back into place.

'I know.' Two words when he knew exactly what she was thinking. One of the few times when he seemed able to read her mind and gauge her feelings. She had been excitedly telling him about her great opportunity and in return she had got his blank wall of silence.

Sooner or later he would have to tell her, and the prospect of that made him frown grimly. Now was not the time. But soon. When she had settled into her job and would accept what he had to say with equanimity, maybe even amusement.

That made him relax. Although he made sure not to prolong the conversation about her job and the fabulous new development that she would be marketing, along with a team of a dozen others. Instead, he talked about what was going on in London, asked her about the people she had worked with at the nightclub, whether she missed any of them, had kept in contact with them, and eventually found the tension oozing out of his body. The *unnecessary* tension, he hastened to add to himself.

The development was looming ahead of them, dominating the skyline and gloriously irreverent in its modernity.

They drove through an arch straight into the courtyard, which was bordered by ranks of car-parking spaces.

'Which apartment?' he asked, looking at the building

with professional satisfaction. 'Right.' He turned to her.
'You go up. George and I will follow with your things.'

Mattie knew better than to launch into the familiar
riposte. Besides, she was dying to see this apartment. It
represented so much more than four walls and a roof
over her head. It was the start of her bright new life, the
one she had been hankering for ever since she was nineteen and old enough to realise just how naïve she had
been in ditching her education in favour of being a mem-
ber of the cool set.

She was still enthusiastically surveying her domain
when the final battered suitcase was deposited on the
floor.

'Isn't it fantastic?' She walked over to the window
and looked down on a stunning vista of sprawling city,
river, bridges, cars and people that looked like moving
toys.

'Where on earth are you going to sleep?'

At this, Mattie turned around and looked at him as
though he had taken leave of his senses.

'On the floor, of course. As you can see, there's no
furniture and I had none to bring with me.'

'The floor.' His expression was rich with distaste and
incredulity.

'In a sleeping bag,' Mattie elaborated, waving her arm
vaguely in the direction of some of her possessions. 'Old
but serviceable. And I took a pillow. I'd offer you some
coffee, but unfortunately no kettle. Or, for that matter,
coffee. And there's no point standing there looking as
though you've been transported into a horror movie. *You*
may find the thought of a sleeping bag inconceivable,
but I don't.'

'Well, you might once you've climbed into one and
discovered that the floor can be harder than you think.'

It hadn't occurred to him that the apartment would be unfurnished. He should have insisted she stay with him until they could equip her with at least a few rudimentary sticks of furniture. Then he wondered what the hell he was thinking. *Stay with him?* He almost laughed aloud at the ludicrous thought that had popped into his head. Not even Rosalind had featured as a possible candidate for sharing his place.

'I happen to know how sleeping bags function, Dominic.' Mattie folded her arms and perched on the sill of the impressive bay window so that she could look at him wryly. 'I've spent many a holiday camping out, though I don't suppose *you* have.' Funny, but it was getting harder and harder to build their differences into the equation. Just as well the odd remark like that surfaced, so that she could be reminded of just how incompatible they were on the most fundamental level.

'We'll have to get you some furniture,' was his response, as he continued to look around him. 'You can't be expected to live like this. Why didn't you take a few more things from the house?' he demanded, finally settling his gaze on her.

'Because none of it belonged to me? Because I could have been accused of theft?'

'And he never offered you anything? Even though you were lovers and you spent years bailing him out of penury by paying the bills?' His mouth curled in disgust. 'We can go to Harrods, get one or two things. Some chairs. A table. A tel—'

'Hold it!' Did he think that he could somehow *buy* her? Because that was what it suddenly felt like. Lust was one thing. But having anything bought for her was out of the question. Those were things that related to a whole different world from the one they had agreed to share. She had a dizzying feeling of wondering what it would be like to be given things out of love, and was momentarily frightened by the power it wove over her. Then she blinked and returned to normal.

'You won't be *buying me* anything. If I want anything, then I'll do what the rest of the human race does. I'll save up.'

'For heaven's sake, Mattie, I can affor—'

'Forget it. I won't accept anything from you and I won't live thinking that you've somehow managed to buy me.'

Dominic saw the determined glint in her eyes and lowered his. He wouldn't allow himself to think of the potential mess that might be the result of his own creating. No. He would sort that out when the time was right. He had never had a problem sorting anything out in his life before.

'OK,' he agreed, his expression changing to one of lazy sensuality. 'Would lunch pass your pride test, in that case?'

Mattie felt herself smile slightly.

'Followed by a housewarming party for two back here?'

How could she resist? She had been so strong when she had first met him. Had known that he was an alien from a different planet. When had he developed that talent for turning her brain to cotton wool? And how long, she wondered with a stirring of alarm, before she discovered that she had no immune system left when it came to him?

CHAPTER SEVEN

'IT'S absolutely fantastic. Meeting prospective clients. Working with the advertising people on ways of making the apartments irresistible to professionals who would rather live north of the river. And have I told you about the ideas we were throwing around for renting out one of the rooms off the atrium as a restaurant? Maybe try wooing one of those celebrity chefs to set it up and get it running?'

No, she hadn't. Dominic pushed back his chair and looked at her with an amused and, he knew, proprietorial smile. This new Mattie was eager, self-confident. Only now and again did the defensive, wary creature rear her head. In about two hours she would be doing that because he would, as he always did, suggest that she stay the night with him instead of going back to her apartment even though, after three weeks, she had at least managed to get herself a bed, a functioning, very small fridge and a small pine table for the kitchen along with two chairs.

'You're not listening to a word I'm saying,' Mattie grumbled. She stood up and began transferring plates and cutlery from table to sink. They now ate here, at his apartment, more often than not. Which, after a month, was still only three nights a week, but three nights that she now found herself looking forward to and expecting with craven anticipation.

'I thought we might go to the country tomorrow. Spend the weekend there. I need to check up on my

119

house there anyway, make sure everything's ticking over.' Dominic clasped his hands behind his head and surveyed her through hooded eyes. How he enjoyed watching her! Watching the way her clothes swung around her, knowing that her body was for his enjoyment only, that with one touch he would feel her tremble for him. He thought about undoing the little pearl buttons of her shirt, softly parting it and then basking in the unsurpassed pleasure of scooping her breasts free of their lacy restraints. He forced himself away from the evocative image to find her staring at him and frowning, perched with her back to the sink.

'There's no need to look at me like that,' he said irritably. 'It's a simple enough suggestion. Get out of London for a weekend, have a break in the country. People do it all the time.' He pushed himself away from the table and went to where she was still standing in thoughtful silence.

'What's there to think about?' He leant over her, hands on either side, propping himself up against the counter. Sheer frustration was beginning to set in. 'This isn't a life or death choice.'

'It wouldn't be a good idea.'

'Why not?' Dominic demanded, frowning darkly. 'I happen to think it's an exceptional idea. When was the last time you got out of London? Went anywhere?'

'That's not the point, Dominic.' Mattie wasn't too sure what the point was but she knew that there was one. He was fond of getting his own way and had a variety of methods for doing just that. He could be as persuasive and as tempting as the devil, could argue her into silent acquiescence if she let him.

'Well? When?'

That, she had learnt to recognise, was another of his

tactics. To simply ignore objections and pursue his own line of questioning until he got what he wanted.

'I can't remember,' Mattie sighed. 'Go and sit back down. I can't think straight when you're looming over me like this.'

'Good. I don't want you thinking straight when you're with me.'

'You're acting like a spoiled child.'

'What...?' Dominic gaped at her in real incredulity. *A spoiled child?* Never before had that accusation been thrown at him. Ever. He clicked his fingers and people snapped to attention. It had always been that way, or for as long as he could remember anyway. For heaven's sake, he hardly ever raised his voice, never mind behaving like a spoiled child!

'Because you want something, doesn't mean it's automatically going to work that way. I thought you would have realised that by now.' Convincing words, but Mattie had to keep her eyes very firmly glued to his. If they so much as wandered a little lower, to his beautiful mouth, there was a very good chance she would be lost, and she had to stand up for herself or end up drowning in this so-called no-strings-attached affair that was not destined to last beyond a few months at the most.

He had made that perfectly clear from the beginning and it didn't take a rocket scientist to work out that he would stick to his guns, his conscience clear when things finally and inevitably ended because hadn't he warned her from the outset that he wasn't interested in commitment on any level?

Never did they project plans that spanned into the future. They saw one another, enjoyed one another, planned something maybe a couple of days down the line, but anything further was out of bounds.

Mattie regularly told herself that his concentration on the present was just what she needed. She had spent years living in some never-never future. First with Frankie and all his dreams about being rich and famous, then with the course, always working hard towards something hovering on the distant horizon.

She knew that it was a breath of fresh air just doing what all other girls her age would be doing. Taking life one day at a time.

'We need to talk about this,' Dominic growled, pushing himself away and striding purposefully into the open-plan sitting area, where he took up fulminating residence on the long, low sofa.

Mattie reluctantly followed.

'I have too much to do to go away for a weekend,' she opened, sitting towards the end of the sofa, one leg lazily tucked under her, the other hanging over the side.

'What?'

'I want to go and have a look for a television. Just a portable thing.'

'You don't need to buy a television,' Dominic asserted arrogantly. 'There are two in this apartment. If you want to watch TV, you can always come here.'

'Now you're being ridiculous.'

'Or you could just take one of mine. OK, *borrow* one of mine. Whatever. That can wait for the duration of one weekend.' He found the thought of visiting his country house without her by his side strangely unappealing. Far from holding the promise of two days of pleasurable solitude, as it normally did, it offered the prospect of unwelcome isolation.

And he really had to go up and check it out. Sylvia, his old retainer, who shared the upkeep of the place with her husband and lived on the premises, had called him two days previously and, having spent five minutes apologising for interrupting him, informed him that there had been a serious leak in one of the downstairs rooms. The plumber had been but there was the question of insurance to sort out, part of the wooden floor had been ruined and the offending radiator would have to be replaced.

'I thought you *liked* going up there on your own.'

'Did I say that?'

'Yes. You told me that it was the one place in the world where you could escape the mad pace and just relax with a book. In fact, you said that you never even went there with your laptop because it was a complete getaway.'

Dominic flushed darkly and scowled. 'I just wanted to give you a break,' he said. He looked down, closing her out for a second, then back at her. 'You can't accuse me of not thinking of you.'

Mattie's heart seemed to halt in mid-beat, then race forward at frantic speed. This was the closest he had ever got to suggesting that what she thought and said and did affected him in any way, and stupidly she found herself clinging to his passing comment until she told herself to just get control of her badly behaved mind.

'OK. I won't.'

For some reason, Dominic felt unreasonably riled at that quick, placating response and his expression darkened.

'Remind me never to suggest something as complicated as a holiday with you,' he intoned tautly. 'You might just go into a coma at the thought of it.'

'A holiday?' she couldn't help saying a little numbly.

'Something that people occasionally go on, usually when they want to spend some time together.' He knew he should retreat while he was ahead but for some reason he wanted to plough on. Yes, so he could turn her on like a light bulb. It was no more than she could achieve with him! Their bodies were made for one another!

But what else? he wondered.

'I know what a holiday is.' Mattie laughed, making light of their conversation.

'Had a lot of them, have you?'

'You know I haven't.'

'Oh, yes. I'd forgotten you worked while studying to make sure the bills got paid while lover boy lazed around, criticised you and drank whatever money was left.'

Mattie chose to disregard his remarks about Frankie. She sometimes wondered how someone could be so thoroughly a part of her past and yet still rear his head at the most unlikely moments.

'I used to go to Cornwall when I was a child,' she confided a little wistfully. She drew her knees up and looked at him with faraway eyes. 'Two weeks over summer to a caravan site. One of those places where the caravans stay in the same place from year to year. You know?'

'Not really.'

'No, I don't suppose you do. I can't picture you in one anyway.' She tried to and failed.

'And I can't much picture you in one either,' Dominic said wryly. 'No, I picture you more on a beach somewhere. White sand, clear warm water, just a whisper of a breeze…an island made for two. And a house with all the trappings. Old wooden floors, mosquito nets over the bed, big windows sprawling open to let the night air waft through…'

Mattie could see it all in her mind's eye and her mouth fell open at the imaginary scenario.

'Holed up with enough food to last the duration, but a little boat moored on the jetty just in case we needed something on the mainland...'

It was the *we* that snapped her back to the present and away from the land of fiction he was leading her confidently into.

'And did you take Rosalind there?' she asked, dipping her eyes.

'Never even crossed my mind,' Dominic said truthfully. What he could have added was that holidaying with women was not something he had ever practised. He had been skiing as a group, in which his current girlfriend might be included, but beyond that his holidays had mostly centred around returning to Greece to see his family. He just worked too damn hard to afford the time off to relax somewhere exotic and remote.

As he had said to her, his weekends in the country were his only real retreats from his working life.

'How come?'

'To start with, because I couldn't take the time off work. And then, later, I wouldn't have wanted to anyway.' He shrugged. 'I don't like talking to you when you're sitting all the way over there,' he said in a husky, coaxing voice. 'Come over here.' He patted the space right by him and Mattie crawled over and collapsed in front of him, her back to his chest, her head finding the hollow between his neck and shoulder.

There was something possessive and familiar about the way he slung his arm around her, the way she slotted so neatly between his legs. She wanted to purr with feline pleasure.

'A man like you should never plan holidays with women,' Mattie said a little ruefully.

'And why would that be?'

'Because by the time the holiday came round, there'd be a good chance that you would have gone off the woman in question.'

'Which brings me back to a weekend in the country. I can guarantee that by tomorrow I won't have gone off you.' He began undoing the little pearl buttons, taking his time. 'Shirts like this should only be worn by confirmed spinsters,' he muttered, and her smile somehow managed to transfer itself to him even though he couldn't see her face.

'And why would that be?'

'Because, my darling, no one would be interested in getting into them.'

Mattie felt a surge of pure, honeyed warmth seep through her and she squirmed against him, tempted to hurry up the whole process of getting undressed by undoing the tricky little buttons herself.

'Say you'll come with me tomorrow,' he murmured into her ear and Mattie reached up to clasp her hands behind his head, her breasts jutting forward with the movement.

Dominic groaned and fumbled with the last stubborn button, almost ripping it off in frustration in the process. Then he unhooked her bra from behind and shoved it up and over the creamy orbs with their pouting pink nipples.

Mattie didn't answer. When he touched her like this, she always found that she couldn't think properly. He was massaging her breasts with both his big hands. She looked down and saw them on her body, the tensile strength of his fingers as they played over her. When he shifted his weight so that he could reach further down and undo the button of her black trousers, quickly followed by the zip, Mattie almost gasped.

Her legs parted automatically. With him, she had no inhibitions. She closed her eyes as his fingers slipped beneath her underwear to slide along that throbbing crease that was wetly awaiting his touch.

He stopped and she nearly groaned in frustration. 'Mattie, look at me.'

She swivelled reluctantly around so that she was looking right at him.

'I want you to come with me this weekend and I don't understand what you're so reluctant about.' He inclined down to deliver a chaste kiss to her lips before straightening back into position.

'We've never slept together.'

'*Never slept together?* Good heavens, woman, what have we been doing with glorious abandon for weeks?'

'No, I meant we've never spent the night together. You know what I mean. Fallen asleep and woken up the following morning in the same bed, next to one another.'

'Not for want of me trying.'

'I just don't think it's such a good idea.'

'You can't make statements like that without benefit of an explanation.' Like a dog with a bone, he wanted her to try and tell him what her reservations were, simply because he knew that he would be able to repudiate them. Naturally this was a relationship based on freedom and mutual attraction, but still, he felt driven to have her do more with him than she seemed willing to do. Why he felt his way, he had no idea. He could only put it down to some hitherto unknown stubborn streak in him that was compelled to gain entry to what appeared out of bounds.

And there were too many out-of-bound areas in this woman for his liking.

Yes, he hated possessiveness in a woman, but did she

have to treat him with such relentless, blithe, cheery *detachment*?

'Are you scared of spending one night with me?' he enquired silkily and Mattie flushed.

'Should I be? Do you turn into a werewolf at midnight?'

'Try me. It's a very pleasing country house. Very quiet up there. Nothing like London. No crowds or tourists. No hailing cabs to get from A to B. Or, in your case, using underground trains, as you enjoy telling me.'

'Well, I *was* planning to doing a little work tomorrow morning. Before I went on my television search…'

'Work?' Dominic paused and then inhaled deeply. 'Aren't you taking this job-commitment thing a little too far?'

'*You* work all the hours God made, if I'm not mistaken.'

'That's different,' he muttered uncomfortably.

'Why? Because your job is so much more high-powered than mine is? I know I'm starting at the bottom of the ladder, but honestly, Dominic, I feel I can really go places.' She propped herself up so that she could look at him properly and was touched to see that he had reddened slightly. 'Try not to forget that this is all new to me,' she persisted gently. 'I want to make a mark and it's hardly as though I have to travel to the ends of the earth to get to work! It's a matter of minutes to walk from my apartment to the conference room they're using on the ground floor!'

'Look,' Dominic said gruffly, 'there's something I feel I ought to tell you…'

'But I only intend to work for about an hour or so. I told Liz that I could pop in and finish off some of the accounts she was doing for the promotion on the bill-boards by Charing Cross...'

Would one weekend away hurt? Walking away from him whenever they spent a night together was struggle enough. Where was the crime in allowing herself the luxury of some time out? She had had barely any rest to speak of between all the work to get her qualification and yet more work to prove to herself and Liz Harris, who had employed her, that she could do whatever was required of her.

'It's about your job...'

'I know it's demanding but I *like* it, I enjoy the pace. OK,' Mattie smiled slowly, 'I'll come with you. Give me an hour and a half, say, to do what I have to do and then you can come and pick me up.'

Which still left what he had to tell her unsaid. Dominic smiled back. He'd spill the beans once the weekend was over. She would be relaxed, they'd both be relaxed.

'Satisfied?' Mattie smiled slowly and seductively at him. She felt expansive all of a sudden and radiantly happy at the prospect of spending a whole lazy weekend with him.

She almost wished, the following morning, that she hadn't promised to put in a couple of hours of work. She packed her bag, threw in some underwear, one change of clothes and nightwear, which would probably be re-dundant.

If the office wasn't, as she had told him, literally a short walk across the building, she might even have been tempted to abandon her generous offer made to Liz two days before, but she would get it out of the way as quickly as possible.

After all, this career, which was still sparkling new

and full of promise, was the one constant in her life. Dominic would go and she would need her work to fill the void.

She let herself into the room soundlessly, enjoying the silence, made herself a cup of coffee and went into the sectioned room that Liz used.

Dominic Drecos, not a million miles away, couldn't concentrate on the figures blinking at him on the computer that was neatly tucked away in the small office he had created from one of the bedrooms in his apartment.

He found his attention drifting from his chief accountant's earnest reports about profit margins to the woman who would be waiting for him at her apartment in precisely forty-five minutes' time.

Eventually he abandoned his attempts to work and resorted to stalking through his apartment, pausing to peer impatiently out of the windows and consult his watch.

He felt like a kid on his first date. When it came to her, he *always* felt like a kid on his first date. Naturally, the novelty wouldn't last. When did things like that ever last? But he was more than happy to go along for the ride and see how far it took him.

He raked long fingers through his dark hair and looked absently down at the street below, propping himself up on the broad window ledge.

It would have done wonders for his conscience if he hadn't known what she was doing right now. Working. Putting in the hard graft that he had instinctively known from the very beginning she would have been capable of. Unfortunately, her putting in hard graft just made him uncomfortably aware that the little talk he had been meaning to have with her for some time now was well behind its due date.

It was a relief to get away from that uncomfortable line of thinking when he glanced at his watch for the eighth time and realised that he could set off to collect her. He would be sure to get held up in traffic and if he didn't, well, he would only be a little early.

On the way, he visualised her reaction to his country house when they got there. It really was very charming. Nothing big and ostentatious. She'd have no reason to round on him in that bull-terrier way of hers, hands on her hips, colour in her cheeks, in full flow about their different backgrounds.

Although... He grinned and the sticky business of talking to her about the job faded into the background. Although lately her pithy little remarks were beginning to seem quite endearing. Maybe he would show her the outdoor Jacuzzi, which would be guaranteed to really get her going. Then, when she was hot under the collar, he could introduce her to the joys of lazing in bubbling warm water with a bottle of chilled wine between them...

Which meant that he was ever so slightly irritated to arrive promptly at her flat, only to discover after ringing the doorbell repeatedly that she wasn't in.

Obviously, the prospect of spending the weekend with him had not filled her with quite the same level of anticipation.

Nor did he know precisely where she was in the building. Nor was there anyone around handy to ask.

His process of elimination took him twenty minutes, during which his irritation levels rose steadily. Head in some damned accounts, he thought impatiently, conveniently forgetting how often in the past he had lost track of time to work.

The door to the office was ajar and Dominic pushed

it open and strode in in one fluid movement, only to find that she wasn't sitting at a desk in front of a computer screen, oblivious to the passage of time and, coincidentally, *him*.

She was by one of the banks of graceful windows that overlooked the inner courtyard, perching on the window sill, and she looked very much as though she had been waiting for him. Which didn't do much to soothe his temper.

'I told you what time I was going to be here, Mattie. What the hell are you still doing in this damned office?' Dominic strode into the room and proceeded to sit, glaring, on one of the polished desks. 'Are you being paid for this volunteered overtime, by the way? I know you want to make a good impression, but believe me some employers can be very cunning when it comes to taking advantage of over-enthusiastic staff.'

'Like you?'

'What?' He had been so caught up in his own irritation that he noticed the expression on her face for the first time, and his dark eyebrows knitted into an impatient frown.

'Like you.' Mattie pushed herself away from the window ledge and walked very steadily, admirably steadily in fact, towards her own desk, taking up position on the black swivel chair so that she could face him. 'Because if it's one thing you are, it's cunning. Am I right or wrong?' She clasped her fingers together and willed him not to come too close to her. She didn't want her body playing its usual pathetic games with her head.

'What are you talking about, Mattie?' He raked his fingers through his hair, although caution was setting in. 'You certainly plan your attacks with lousy timing. We're about to spend a weekend together and neither of us needs to kick off with an argument. So to nip this in the bud, I *don't* happen to be the sort of employer who takes advantage of his employees.' That didn't seem to have nipped anything in the bud. She was still looking at him as if he was something that had crawled out from under a rock.

'Finished here?' Dominic tried to sound reasonably jovial, although it was a struggle. 'Or still got one or two stray accounts you want to wrap up some time to-day?' That little bit of sarcasm slipped out. It didn't meet with the amused smile that usually greeted his frequent bouts of sarcasm, the one he had become accustomed to. In fact, it met with a wall of reinforced steel.

'Actually, I finished the accounts quite a while ago.' Then, 'And you wouldn't believe just how interesting the process was.'

'What's going on here, Mattie? Care to tell me? Or are we going to talk in riddles for the next two hours while I try and get to the bottom of whatever it is you want to say?'

'Since I've been working here, I really haven't got involved in the accounts side of things at all. I've really just been tagging along with the marketing crew, dealing with stuff from prospective clients.'

'And you sound overjoyed at being given additional responsibility. If that responsibility happens to materi-alise on a Saturday morning when we're planning on driving up to the country, then who am I to complain?'

'But I made a very interesting discovery this morning while I was innocently rooting through the filing cabinet in Liz's office in search of some files I needed.' Sitting down put her at a disadvantage for this conversation but she couldn't trust her legs if she got up.

'Oh? And what was that?' Dominic's black eyes narrowed on her face. Her highly unreadable face, and he felt a sudden, sharp stirring of deep unease.

'Your connection with this particular group of people who have been hired to cover the marketing for the development.' Mattie watched his face very carefully and knew she was looking for something, some little sign that would tell her just how off target she was. No such sign. In fact, she saw him flush darkly and knew that the assumptions she had made had been spot-on.

He had manipulated her in the worst way possible. He had manoeuvred for her to get this job and, with it, the flat.

And she knew why he had done it. He had wanted her from the moment he had set eyes on her and, in his usual arrogant way, he had simply taken measures to ensure that he got what he wanted. Frankie was around, and so what better way to make sure that that inconvenience was sorted than by getting her a job in which accommodation was part of the package? He wanted her away from the dangerous divide that she had persisted in creating, and so he had simply found her a job that would elevate her into a career woman capable of stepping over the chip on her shoulder that had been holding her back.

She felt tears threaten and clenched her jaw accordingly.

'I found a letter from you stuck at the bottom of a file congratulating Bob Hodge on acquiring the building, asking him to keep you informed as to what he was going to do with it.' She could hear herself pleading with him for a denial that didn't come.

'So what did you do, Dominic?' she whispered. 'Called in a favour? Asked him to make a space in his qualified team so that I could be slotted in? Like an imbecile who wasn't capable of finding a job for herself? How could you? How could you have manipulated my life like that?'

'I wasn't manipulating your life, Mattie.' Hadn't he been?

'Oh, right! You once told me that you always got what you wanted. Were you just making sure that you got what you wanted even if the route was a little underhand?' Her voice was trembling with disappointment and anger, and when he made as though to move towards her she turned away in immediate rejection.

'OK, maybe I went around things the wrong way, and maybe I should have told you from the start that I could have got you this job, but would you have listened? Or would you have jumped on your bandwagon and denied yourself the opportunity just to be pigheaded?'

'That's not the point!'

'You haven't answered my question!'

'I wanted to do things on my own. I didn't need any help from you!'

'You're acting as though somehow I've committed a crime against your pride, Mattie. But how far does pride really get any of us?'

'Stop trying to twist everything around so that you can emerge in a positive light.' It scared her how badly she wanted him to succeed. 'You manipulated me. That's all there is to it.'

Dominic smashed his fist down on the desk and a little container of pens and paper clips toppled over and spilled. Mattie looked at it in mute fascination.

'That is *not* all there is to it, dammit!' This time her icy expression wasn't enough to deter him and he covered the distance between them in a few furious seconds. 'So maybe I wasn't as upfront as I should have been—'

'Understatement of the year!' She pressed back into the chair to try and avoid his towering presence from engulfing her totally.

'If I was trying to manipulate you, wouldn't I have *told* you about the job?' Dominic demanded, his face so close to hers that she could see straight into the black depths of his eyes. 'Wouldn't I have jumped at the first chance to make you feel that you owed me? I damn well didn't do that, did I?'

'Well, maybe you were just saving that as your trump card!' Mattie flared back. 'Something you could pull out of your sleeve if the occasion ever arose and you needed to! Pulling strings! That's all you're good at, isn't it, Dominic? Just as you pulled strings with Harry to get to meet me in the first place! You think that everyone should dance to your tune and it's…it's *hateful*!'

There was a charged silence and abruptly he stood up and walked away, towards the very same window against which she had been standing when he had first entered the room.

'I tried to tell you—'

'When?' Mattie demanded shrilly. She swivelled the chair so that she was looking at him.

'Yesterday. I told you we needed to talk about your job. Then things got carried away and I figured I'd tell you after the weekend.'

Yes, she did remember him saying something along those lines. And no, the last thing she wanted to think about was how they had become carried away. Getting carried away had been her big mistake from the word go.

'I don't believe you, Dominic,' she said quietly. 'You wanted me so you took the necessary steps to get me. You never spared a thought for my feelings because you don't know the meaning of the word *sensitivity*.' Her voice thickened with bitterness. 'That's what our whole relationship was about. Lust. Want. Sex. No feelings anywhere in the equation.'

'It's what *you* wanted as well, or have you decided to conveniently forget that?'

No, she hadn't. She'd just made the simple mistake of forgetting to hang on to the original deal they had struck. Because now it felt like a deal. Two people, neither wanting involvement, just giving in to their baser instincts with the unspoken agreement that it would never progress from there. It had been a rubbish deal and she could see that now, because somewhere along the way she had made the fatal error of liking him, then falling slowly in love with him.

It was a hideous realisation. Mattie closed her eyes briefly in despair. When she opened them again, there was a new hardness there.

'There's no point discussing this further, Dominic.' She placed one hand flat on the desk and stood up, moving to stand behind it so that it was a physical and significant barrier between them. 'I don't like what you did. And I can't respect anyone who would behave like that. This relationship, or whatever it was, was never going anywhere and now I'm bringing it to an end.' She afforded him a view of her ramrod-straight back as she turned to face one of the windows. Her heart longed to see him one last time. Her head refused to allow her the luxury.

But she knew he hesitated. Heard it as she followed his footsteps to the door, the brief pause. Then it was all over and he was gone.

CHAPTER EIGHT

GLORIA had gone home. Dominic had given her the afternoon off in a fit of grudging compassion. The poor woman had been reduced to tiptoeing around him for the past fortnight as his temper had become increasingly vile. She had arrived every morning to find him already at his desk, head buried in his work, only looking up when she entered to mutter the barest of greetings. Instructions had been given to her with deadly abruptness and he knew that he had been a snarling beast on the odd occasion when his plans for the day had been unexpectedly disrupted.

Dominic liked his secretary. The last thing he wanted was to drive her to the furthest reaches of her patience.

On the other hand, he just couldn't seem to help himself. He couldn't get Mattie out of his head, or the way their affair had ended. With a dismissive little parting shot that managed to sum him up as some kind of monstrous, self-serving opportunist who had availed himself of whatever weapons he possessed in his armoury in an attempt to bed her.

He had replayed that last conversation so many times in his head that he thought he was going crazy.

But not as many times as he had stood by his office window, when his computer was going mad and his phone lines were buzzing, thinking about whether he should go and see her. Corner her in her office.

He was doing it right now. At six-thirty in the evening, when he should be taking advantage of the relative peace to answer the growing mound of correspondence that needed seeing to. Standing by the window, scowling and cursing himself for the way she had climbed under his skin and wrapped herself round his heart. His so-called deadened heart that had supposedly learnt lessons from past experience.

With a muffled oath Dominic began pacing his office, like a panther trapped in a cage when the rest of the jungle was calling him outside.

If he went to see her, then what? Another argument, with the same result, but this time conducted in full view of her work colleagues? He certainly couldn't confront her in her apartment because she had moved out. Gone where, he had no idea. Probably back to the ex. Just the thought of that was enough to make him swear profusely to himself.

His big mistake had been to telephone Liz Harris, her boss, on the pretext of trying to locate *her* boss, and then engage himself casually on the subject of Mattie, how she was doing in the job, how she liked the apartment. Which was when he had discovered that she had moved out.

That had been five days ago. Five very bad days during which he had had ample time to realise that not seeing her was on a par with a slow, painful death and thinking of her back in the arms of Frankie was even worse. Five nightmare nights during which he had been forced to accept that what had started as a casual fling had ended up as a deadly serious relationship that he had thrown away like an idiot.

He veered wildly from cursing himself for not having been honest with her from the word go, to raging at her for having taken his involvement in the wrong light.

He had already snatched his jacket from the cabinet

in which it was stored, along with a change of suit and several shirts, and was sticking it on when the phone rang.

Dominic let it ring, debating whether his mood could carry him through yet another meaningless call with a client, and eventually decided that he really couldn't let work suffer at the expense of what he was going through.

Not that Mattie was in the slightest bit aware of the argument going on in his head as she waited tensely on the other end of the line. The only thing she was aware of was the frantic beating of her heart and the acute nervousness that was making her perspire just at the thought of hearing his voice.

She almost dropped the mobile phone when she finally did hear that voice snap shortly down the line, which made her wonder whether she had caught him on the way out, which in turn made her head spin with the possibilities of where exactly he was on his way out *to*.

Don't even go there, she told herself feverishly, as if she hadn't been there a thousand times and back over the past fortnight.

'Hello, Dominic, it's me. Mattie.' Her voice was as controlled as her feelings were not.

He heard the coolness in her voice and all thoughts of his part in the dissolution of their relationship vanished like a puff of smoke. Back came the irrational anger that he had been ditched, *ditched,* by someone whom he had done the biggest favour possible, sorted out her career.

He should inform her in a few pithy phrases that he wanted nothing further to do with her. His pride demanded it.

Dominic moved over to his desk, sat down and swivelled around so that he was facing the window.

'Yes?' His voice was equally cold.

'Have I caught you on your way out?' Mattie asked and when he told her that, as a matter of fact she had, she immediately and again wildly wondered where he had been planning on going. Bad move. She needed her wits about her to get through this call, not scattered to the four winds because jealousy was eating away at her like a poison.

'What do you want?' Dominic asked flatly.

'We need to talk.'

'Really?' He stared out into the nothingness that sprawled outside his window and felt a surge of heady excitement made all the more powerful by the fact that he hadn't been the one to initiate the contact. But hell, her voice sounded good. 'What about? More of the same? Or have you come to your senses and realised that I might actually have had a valid point of view, after all?'

'Where were you going tonight? Somewhere important? Anything you could cancel? I really would like to see you sooner rather than later.' Her words came out in a rush and she found that she was still holding her breath while the seconds ticked by.

'I suppose I could cancel my…appointment.' What appointment? The only appointment he had was a date with the bottle of whisky back in his apartment and the television with the sound turned down. 'I could come over to the apartment, I guess…'

'I've moved out.'

Dominic simulated astonishment. She would have a field-day if she knew that he had phoned her boss to enquire about her and sheer pride refused to allow her that option. 'Moved out? Where to? No, let me guess. Back to that loser of a boyfriend of yours, I expect. Running back to what you know even if it's bad for your health.'

Mattie couldn't help herself. 'And do you think that *you* were good for my health, Dominic? Lying and cheating your way into my…into my bed.' *Into my heart,* she nearly said, only biting back the dangerous words at the last minute.

'Is that why we need to talk, Mattie? So that you can throw a few more accusations my way? Because if it is…' If it was, well, he still wanted to see her, Dominic thought with disgust.

'No.' Mattie spoke quickly, already regretting her outburst. There was no place for that and she didn't want to be distracted down that road.

She had had long enough to dwell on what he had done and yes, she was still furious with him, but under the fury was a niggling admission that he had really helped her. It was help that she would have rejected out of hand had he told her his intentions from the start.

The job suited her perfectly. It was challenging and well-paid and she enjoyed the people she worked with. She would never have landed on her feet like that without him. And like it or not, he had had a point when he had told her that had he really wanted to manipulate her, he would have dangled that particular carrot in his hand.

'So…you still haven't said.' It irked him to flog this particular horse but, dammit, he had to know.

'Haven't said what?'

'Where you're living now, if you've left the apartment.'

'I haven't gone back to Frankie's,' Mattie said reluctantly. 'Actually, I've found somewhere near

Wimbledon. It's small and not in the best of areas, but it does, and the rent's a lot cheaper than I would be paying in central London.'

Dominic felt himself literally shudder in relief. 'Where are you now?' he asked, prepared to be magnanimous now that that particular nightmare scenario, the one where she was back with her ex and loving every minute of it, had been dispelled.

'In that bistro two blocks away from where your office is, as a matter of fact.'

That came as a surprise. Dominic turned away from the window and slowly drew his chair up to the desk. 'You mean you went to that bistro on the off-chance that I would be able to meet you there when you called?'

'It seemed as good a place as any.' Mattie glanced around. There was a fair amount of people filling it, all still in their work clothes. This wasn't the sort of place where people went to get drunk. They had a couple of glasses of wine, maybe, something light to eat, but no rowdiness. Just the comfortable safety of people around. 'I've got a table at the back. Will you be able to make it?'

'I'll be there in ten minutes.'

Oh, yes, the world suddenly seemed a glorious place, filled with light and colour and…possibilities. Dominic shrugged on his jacket and almost whistled in the elevator down to Reception. His car was in the basement, but no need to take it when the wine bar was within walking distance.

She was there. *Waiting for him!* True, she had sounded a little cold on the telephone, but that could have been the reception. Mobile phones distorted voices and she would have been using her mobile, the one thing she had accepted from him because he had insisted on her having it. Knowing that she was safe because of that damned underground system she refused to abandon in favour of the taxi. He could remember the way she had looked at him and grinned when he had pressed it into her hand and then, over lunch, patiently showed her how to use it.

The fact was that she had called him, wanted to see him. They would talk, not in an atmosphere of anger as they had the last time, but cautiously, taking steps to iron out the misunderstandings. And he was prepared to do anything to iron out those misunderstandings because he couldn't imagine life without her.

He made it to the wine bar in record time.

And there she was, as promised, sitting primly at the table at the back, wearing a dark grey dress and a black jacket. Dominic took a few pleasurable seconds just looking at her as she stared thoughtfully at the glass in front of her, tracing the circular rim with one finger.

She looked up just at that moment and their eyes met. Only for a few seconds, but he got the impression that dashing over to him and flinging her arms around him was not going to happen. Which made him walk rather more warily towards her than he felt like doing.

'That was quick.' Mattie gave him a tense, unrevealing smile. 'I didn't expect you so soon.'

'I said ten minutes.'

'I thought you might have had to get in touch with whoever you were meeting. Cancel whatever arrangements you'd made.'

Still the same bland politeness that he hadn't wanted or, for that matter, expected. Still standing, Dominic glanced at the bar and then back to her. 'I'm going to get myself a drink. What do you want? What are you drinking?'

'Just mineral water, and no, I'm fine.'

'Food? Shall I bring a couple of menus?' Talking like strangers. He didn't want this, but he would let her take her time to get where she wanted. Which had to be *them*, back together, or why else would she have made contact at all? It couldn't have been easy.

'Sure. Why not?' Mattie shrugged and looked away. 'Actually, you can order for me. Just some fish would be fine.'

Which he did, returning to the table a few minutes later with his drink in one hand and more confusing thoughts than he felt he could handle.

'So, how are you?' he asked, still as polite as hell. He sat down opposite her, cradled his drink for a few seconds before tossing some of it down his throat.

'The job's still brilliant.' Mattie looked at her glass of water, up at him, and then back to the glass. She knew that she had to be very controlled here but it was damned difficult. Seeing him was so much worse than hearing his voice, and hearing his voice had been bad enough.

'Why did you give up the apartment?'

'You know why.'

'I'm surprised you didn't jack the job in as well, in that case.'

'Look, let's get one thing straight. Whatever your motivations were, I love what I'm doing.'

'So I'm not the monster after all?'

'I don't want to talk about that.'

'Then what exactly *do* you want to talk about?' His patience was beginning to wear thin under the strained formalities.

'What have you been doing these past few weeks?' Mattie asked, diverting the subject and not very subtly. She had yearned to see him again, longed for him with every ounce of her foolish, love-struck being. Sure, she had spent hours nursing her bitterness at what he had done, telling herself that she shouldn't be surprised because hadn't she put him down as an arrogant swine from the first moment he had swept into her life? But then she hadn't been in love with him. Which was what was really hurting now. Knowing what he was and still loving him so much that it was like a constant, pressing pain.

And she was scared as well. Scared at what he would be thinking in an hour from now, when she had told him what she had to tell him. Which was why she was more than happy to play for a little time.

'Working hard.' Dominic finished his drink and, as their food was put in front of them, ordered another.

'And playing hard too?'

'Care to define what you mean by playing hard?'

'Forget it.'

'No, I haven't been seeing a bevy of women since you. Is that what you mean? Or would you rather shove me into the role of ruthless womaniser along with everything else? The sort of man who would open door two the minute door one closes?' This wasn't going quite the way he had thought it might and his earlier optimism that they would put their differences behind them was now beginning to bring home to him what a naïve fool he had been.

'I don't want to argue with you.' Mattie dropped her eyes and wondered what it was she was expecting. Or why she had even come. No, she knew why she had come. She fiddled with the food on her plate, shoving it around in useless circles, finally swallowing a mouthful although it tasted like cardboard.

'Which begs the question, what exactly *do* you want?

And why don't we drop the game playing? You're enjoying your job, I'm working hard. How about moving on from that to why you called me out of the blue?'

'Would you have called *me* if I hadn't gotten in touch with you?' Mattie had to ask that. Another taboo question in so far as she knew she wouldn't like the answer, but something still compelled her to ask it.

'You made your position perfectly clear when we last met.' Dominic closed his knife and fork, for once deserted by his reliable, hearty appetite. He couldn't stomach another mouthful of steak, however good it was. In fact, he felt in dire need of another whisky and soda although he knew it wasn't a good idea. 'I was the big, bad wolf who had managed to corner innocent Little Red Riding Hood and, even though he managed to secure her a safe passage through the woods and fix her up in a nifty little weatherproof cottage, he was still the big, bad wolf because he should have told her what he was going to do. Should have given her the opportunity to throw his offer back in his face and face her journey through the woods on her own. Hell, if you think I'm going to tell you that I would have pursued you nevertheless, then you'll be waiting forever.' Pride. Stubborn pride that had slammed back into place. The galling truth was that he would have contacted her. Made up some spurious excuse, but he would have got in touch with her, just because he would have needed to. Like an addict needing his fix.

'Right.'

Her silent acceptance of his statement only fuelled his anger. 'What did you expect me to say?' he pressed, angry with her for the stoniness that had him thrown and angry with himself for not being able to grab hold of some of that legendary self-control for which he was known.

'Nothing. The truth. Which is what you just said.' Mattie picked up her glass of water, realised that her hand was shaking, and immediately put the glass back down on the table.

'I'm glad we understand each other,' she said, meeting his eyes with a steadiness that cost her dear. 'This way, we can discuss what I have to say like adults.'

'Discuss…what?' Dominic was getting more uneasy by the minute.

'I'm pregnant.'

The silence was deafening. It seemed to stretch on and on and on. For hours. If it hadn't been all so deadly serious, she might have laughed, seeing this dangerously beautiful man who was usually never lost for words rendered so utterly speechless.

In fact, this bit of it was really just as she had imagined it would be.

Ever since she had found out herself, which had only been a matter of a few hours before.

Now those few hours seemed like a dream, like an event that had occurred months previously. All the questions she had asked herself in her terrified panic were no longer raging inside her head like demons. She was pregnant and that was simply a *fait accompli*. And lord knew, she would still be ignorant if she hadn't been to see her doctor because she had been feeling tired and putting on weight even though her appetite had vanished.

He had asked her the one question she had never asked herself and of course she had denied it. She couldn't possibly be pregnant. She was on the contraceptive pill!

'I beg your pardon?' Those four words were dropped

like stones into a still pond and Mattie forced herself to meet his eyes calmly. At least, as calmly as she could.

'You heard me. I'm pregnant.'

'You asked me to come *here* to tell me this?' He shoved his plate to one side all the better to lean across the narrow table and close the space between them.

'Would you rather I had never bothered to tell you?' Mattie shot back. 'Believe me, it did cross my mind but then, believe it or not, I do happen to possess one or two moral values...'

'Spare me the trip down hardship lane, Mattie...'

'I'm telling you this because I feel you have a right to know that you've fathered a child. I do apologise if you'd rather I hadn't said anything!'

Mattie had never wondered what she would feel like if she ever discovered that she was pregnant. The truth was that she had never really considered it at all. She knew, though, that this was not how it should be. In an ideal world, she shouldn't be sitting in a bistro breaking this news to a man who wanted a baby about as much as he wanted a rampant dose of the bubonic plague. In an ideal world, she should be sharing this news with joy in her heart to a man who would hold her close and tell her that that was the greatest news he'd ever had.

Unfortunately life was never ideal and hers, in particular, seemed hell-bent on tripping her up.

Not that there wasn't a secret little happiness inside her, growing with each passing minute. A lot of wonder and, underneath the anxiety and doubts and fear, a seed of pleasurable completion was already sending shoots up, making her think how much she wanted this child, conceived in love even if the love was one-sided.

'What I meant is, why did you bring me *here* to break this news? To this place? How are we supposed to conduct a conversation here, surrounded by people and noise?' Dominic looked around him restlessly but then his eyes were back on her face, as if he couldn't tear them away for long enough to even scan the room.

'I thought we might just have a quick chat—'

'*A quick chat!*'

'And then when you've had time to absorb it all, we could maybe meet and discuss things…in a bit more detail. If that's what you want…' Her eyes skittered away from his.

'What do you think I want?'

'Look, Dominic, I know this is a bit of a bombshell…'

'And you once told *me* that I was the master of understatement!'

'It was a shock to me as well.'

In the midst of his swirling confusion, this brought Dominic up short. Yes, it would have been a shock to her. She had only now started on the long, slow climb up the career ladder. To discover that she was pregnant must have been as much of a bombshell to her.

Her powers of recuperation were obviously second to none, he thought a little acidly. Because she certainly didn't look like a woman in a state of shock. She was calm, cool and utterly collected. The hallmarks of a woman relaying information without a shred of emotion to convey what she was really feeling.

'How did it happen?' he asked in an effort to bring some normality to his wildly cavorting emotions. 'Look, I'm going to have to get another drink. Want anything?'

Mattie shook her head and watched him as he walked up to the bar and then stood, restlessly tapping on the counter, while his drink was poured.

She had been right to meet him in a public place. A bit of a cowardly move but a good one, because at least here he couldn't give vent to his obvious temptation to storm at her, which was what he wanted to do. If he raised his voice one decibel she could always walk out, and anyway he wouldn't. His arms were tied with people all around them. He would be forced to discuss this like an adult and she needed him to do that. One wrong word from him and she felt that she might crack. Under the calm exterior, emotions were just waiting to burst their banks and lord only knew what she would say to him if that happened. Tell him that she was *glad* that she was pregnant? Tell him that she had fallen in love with him? Put him in a position where his horror at an admission like that would force him to kindly but politely remind her of the pact they had made, the non-involvement pact that she had broken?

Maybe he might even accuse her of getting pregnant on purpose so that she could drag commitment out of him even though she knew that commitment was the equivalent of a four-letter word to him.

'You asked me how it happened,' Mattie said, as soon as he had sat back down. Polite. Businesslike. Because to him this would be business and not particularly pleasant business. 'I…I came off the Pill for the last six months I was with Frankie. We weren't…and, anyway, I thought it was a good time to give my body a break, so the first time we…well, I wasn't protected. Silly, I know, but I didn't think. By the time I started back using contraception, well, obviously it was too late…and I didn't know because…'

'OK. I get the picture.'

'Look, I'm sorry.' Mattie felt a dismaying sense of unreality and had to struggle to get her thoughts together. 'I know you think that this is probably going to turn your world upside-down, but it won't.'

'And how do you work that one out? Clarify for me.'

You don't even care, do you? she wanted to shout. 'Nothing's going to change between us. It's only right that you should know but it's a formality—'

'A formality!' Dominic banged his fist on the table.

'Ssh!'

'Don't tell me to be quiet, Mattie! You chose this ridiculous venue to break this news, well, you'll just have to live with the fact if I don't collude and duck down quietly!'

'Shouting isn't going to get us anywhere.'

'And what are you proposing we do? What's this *anywhere* you have in mind?'

'Maybe we shouldn't have met here after all,' Mattie whispered, biting her lip. Several people had looked around when his fist had hit the table, and she could feel their ears flapping at the prospect of an impromptu cabaret show even though they had returned to their conversations.

'You picked the place!'

'Could you keep your voice down?'

'I'll shout as loudly as I like!' Dominic deliberately raised his voice a few more notches and was rewarded by sudden silence from the tables surrounding them. Then he sat back and folded his arms and looked at her.

How dared she think that she could be carrying his baby, only to tell him that his involvement was reduced to a mere formality?

She looked pale and tense and he had a sudden urge just to go round the table, pull her to her feet and wrap his arms around her until the paleness and the tension were both wiped away.

'We need to get out of here,' he said roughly. 'This is no place to discuss a subject like this and you know it. We'll go back to my apartment. It's only ten minutes' walk away and at least we'll be private there.'

'No way!' The thought of being alone with him in his apartment, the place where they had shared so many good times, where her love had taken root and grown without her even realising, made her flush with panic. 'If anything, we can go to…to my place. But there's nothing we can say there that we can't say here.' She discovered that she was wringing her hands, like a damsel in some Victorian saga, and she shoved them safely out of sight on her lap.

'Fine.'

Which was not the description she would have used as they sat in total silence in the back of the cab on the way to her flat. Hideous might have been more apt. And if she felt like this now, trapped and miserable and longing for the impossible, when they weren't even alone, how was it going to be when they were in her very tiny sitting room?

It felt like ages before the taxi arrived at the tired converted Victorian house.

'You live *here*?' Dominic asked in a scathing voice. 'You gave up the apartment to move into this?'

'It's affordable,' Mattie said briefly, turning to unlock the front door. She could feel his presence behind her and it sent ripples of awareness shooting up and down her spine like moth wings.

'It would be,' Dominic commented from behind her, looking at the eight little cubby-holes used for the post, 'considering how many people are crammed in here. I suppose you're at the top?'

Mattie ignored him, even though it wasn't too difficult to imagine what he was thinking as they mounted the stairs towards her flat. Peeling wallpaper, threadbare carpet, bare bulbs hanging at intervals from the high ceilings.

'You do realise,' he said, once they were inside her flat and she had shut the door behind them, 'that this is unacceptable.' He stood in the middle of the room and looked around him with a practised and disdainful eye.

'I happen to find it very comfortable.'

'A sitting room with a bed shoved up one end, a bath-room that can only accommodate an anorexic and a kitchen...' he strolled into the kitchen, cast the same disapproving eye around '...a kitchen just about big enough to house a table and two chairs, provided mo-bility isn't high on the list of priorities. It won't do.'

Mattie felt tears spring up into her eyes and she turned away quickly, but not quickly enough.

His arms around her were like a sanctuary and a haven and she turned around into him, feeling his warmth settle over her like a blanket.

'It's not just you now.' His words sank into her hair. 'You're having my baby and I won't let you tackle this pregnancy alone, in a dump like this, never mind when the baby's born.'

'You won't *let* me?' Mattie pushed herself out of the treacherous embrace and walked towards the window, to turn round and face him. 'I didn't come to see you so that you could...could *manipulate* me...again!'

'I don't give a damn what you call it, Mattie, but hear me now and hear me very carefully...' His voice was low and travelled from his mouth to her ears like an arrow, a deadly, speeding arrow. 'You will not bring any child of mine up in a place like this. You will not labour up flights of stairs when you're pregnant, risking a mis-carriage. You might not care for me laying down the law, but that's exactly what I intend to do.'

Mattie's mouth was hanging open. 'B-but why?' she stammered. 'It's not as though…as though this is some kind of love match.' She winced as she said that, hating the cold way it sounded, as though what she had felt for him, and still felt, could be dismissed in a few well-chosen words. 'You misunderstood my intentions in telling you about the pregnancy! I know you never wanted fatherhood.' Good heavens. She knew he could barely bring himself to utter the word *relationship* without adding a string of other qualifications!

'And however strong your sense of duty is, I don't intend to fall victim to it.' Brave words that cost her dear.

Dominic strode over to where she was perched on the window ledge, but instead of doing his usual, trapping her so that the sheer force of his personality could engulf her, he leaned against the window and looked down outside so that she was privy to his averted profile.

'This isn't about *you*, though, is it?' He turned to look at her then. 'And it isn't about whether I wanted to become a daddy or not. The reality is that you're pregnant with my baby and I intend to take care of the situation.'

'This is not *a situation*,' Mattie told him, but a small, treacherous side of her longed to be taken care of. It was the same small, treacherous side that had told her she could handle a man like Dominic. Wisdom would be to avoid that small, treacherous side like the plague.

'Event. Occurrence. Happening. Call it whatever you want to, but whatever you decide to call it you're not running away from me this time.'

Mattie stared at him. Her breathing slowed. Even her heartbeat seemed to have slowed.

'We're going to get married.'

CHAPTER NINE

MATTIE being Mattie, she laughed, walked towards the tired old single bed that she had converted into a sofa of sorts with the addition of three cushions and a colourful throw. She plonked herself down, leaned against the cushions and stretched out her legs.

'Married? What a ridiculous suggestion. We aren't living in the Dark Ages. In case the twenty-first century has passed you by, Dominic, women get pregnant these days and bring the baby up very competently and very single-handedly.' She took one of the cushions and pressed it to her stomach, drawing her legs up so that she was peering at him over her knees.

'Good for them.' Dominic shrugged indifferently. 'Fortunately their lives don't concern me.' He had known what her reaction would be and he was more than prepared to listen to all her objections. But they weren't going to do any good. She would marry him and the thought felt good, right somehow. Fate had given him his hand to play and he intended to play it very well indeed. 'Yours, on the other hand, does.'

Mattie squeezed the cushion to her. Marriage. No emotion, no mention of love. Just another business proposition, just like the one she had been idiotic enough to accept the first time round.

This man could make her burst out laughing, could make her think, could make her body sing with pleasure, could make her fall hopelessly in love with him. He could do all that and still keep that vital part of himself shut away, and now he was proposing marriage. Well, thoroughly modern she might be, but she wasn't so modern that she was going to tie herself up in a loveless union. That spelt days and years of misery, hungering silently for the impossible, becoming the anchor round his ankles that he quietly endured for the sake of his child.

She kind of wished that he would come a bit closer to her instead of just standing there, watching her.

'Look, Dominic…' Mattie's voice took on a coaxing, reasonable tone. 'We both know why we got involved with one another and we both know what the stipulations were. No talk of commitment, never mind marriage.' She wished desperately that she had seen what she could see now. That he had wanted her physically and that he was a man capable of extracting emotion from any situation. Without emotion all things were possible. Even marriage to a woman he fancied, liked even, but did not love.

What had possessed her to imagine that she had access to the same kind of inner coldness that he had? When she had spent years tied up with Frankie because she felt sorry for him? She had no doubt that he could remain married to her forever. To her or to anyone, for that matter, because he would never be victim to the agonising of his feelings. He doubtless envisaged a union wherein he might just carry on sleeping with her till he got bored, then he would simply conduct his private life discreetly outside the marital home. His child would be the one to keep him rooted.

'That was then and this is now.'

'I just can't get married to you. I could never marry anyone unless there was love. Why do you think I never married Frankie? Well, you know. I told you once. I might have stayed with him, might have thought I loved him, and I did in a way, but deep down I knew that I could never marry him because the love wasn't there, not the kind of love that makes a marriage work.'

Dominic gave a short, derisive bark of laughter. 'And what sort of love is that, Mattie? The sort with pink icing on the top?'

'You're so cynical!' Mattie flared back. 'It's the kind of love that keeps my parents together! And yours as well!'

Dominic shrugged. 'They belong to a different generation,' he dismissed. 'Divorce these days is endemic. Married one day, divorced the next.' He stuck his hands casually in the pockets of his trousers and continued to look at her thoughtfully. 'Now here are my thoughts on the matter. We were two people who were attracted to one another, had a relationship, and now you're pregnant with my baby. Yes, on one level I can't deny that everything in my life is about to change. On the other hand, I'm thirty-four years old. Leave it much longer and I might still be capable of fathering a child, but, as they say, would lack the energy to pick it up. I also don't walk away from my responsibilities.'

'I'm not asking you to walk away from anything!' Mattie protested desperately. 'When the baby's born, you can come and visit whenever you want…'

'When the baby's born, there will be no need for that because you will be living with me, under my roof, as my wife. I will not have any child of mine born illegitimate, and don't,' Dominic raised his hand in rejection of the stunned protest Mattie was about to make, 'bother telling me that illegitimacy is the norm these days. Where I come from, babies are born into wedlock.'

'*Happy* wedlock,' Mattie contradicted in a shaking voice.

'Happy wedlock is successful wedlock and we have the ingredients to make it work.' He ticked them off one by one on his fingers. 'One, we like one another. Two, we were great in bed. Three, we are going to have a child and, like it or not, a child needs the support of both parents. Both parents, on tap. Four, without love muddying the waters, our partnership stands an even greater chance of survival.'

This, he knew, was the only way to persuade her. Reason. Cool, calm logic. No mention of his tortured nights when his imagination took flight and refused to come back down to earth. He would deal with all that himself.

'And what when…the *great in bed* bit begins to wane? What then?'

Dominic looked down briefly. Wane? This woman made him feel alive, sensationally so. He seriously couldn't imagine a day when he wouldn't want her or want to be with her.

'Why cross bridges before we get to them?' he asked. 'Now, who have you told about…this? Your parents? Friends?'

Mattie shuddered. Living in sin with Frankie might have scraped through her parents' moral net, but single and pregnant to a man they didn't know and who didn't feature as an ongoing part of her life was a different thing altogether.

'I've only just found out myself!' she objected. 'You're the only other person who knows, and I'm beginning to wonder whether I shouldn't have just kept my mouth shut.'

'I shouldn't if I were you.' Dominic's voice was grim.

'Shouldn't what?'

'Go down the road of thinking what might have happened if you had kept this to yourself. Because sooner or later I would have found out and then your life wouldn't have been worth living.'

'If that is supposed to reassure me that marrying you is the best thing I could do, then you're way off target!'

'Think about it, Mattie. How do you think I would react, how any normal man would react, if he discovered that he'd fathered a child without knowing it? If he suddenly bounced into his ex walking hand in hand with a toddler who was his?'

'A lot of so-called *normal* men would breathe a hearty sigh of relief that they hadn't been landed with the burden of bringing up a child they didn't ask for!' Mattie flashed back at him.

'We could argue about this till the cows came home. No point. When do you intend to tell your parents?'

'Soon,' Mattie told him uncomfortably. She sneaked a glance at him and hated the way just looking at him could make her feel all hot and bothered and hideously aware of her vulnerability.

'And what do you think they're going to say about you living here, pregnant and alone?'

Not a lot, Mattie thought miserably. They certainly wouldn't be clapping their hands with glee. More likely, they would go silent with disappointment and that would be all the harder to bear after their joy at her landing her job. And their relief, even though they had tried hard to hide it down the end of the phone, that she and Frankie were no longer an item.

'Especially when they find out that the father of your child proposed marriage.'

That conjured up an even more disastrous scenario. 'How would they find that out?'

'Well, I would tell them, naturally.'

'That would be emotional blackmail!'

Dominic refrained from informing her that he would use anything to get her back into his life, where she belonged. Not even his pride, which reared up every time he thought about her sleeping with him then dismissing him with a flick of her head, could stop him from still wanting her back, needing her back.

'But of course,' he went on smoothly and relentlessly, like a bulldozer ploughing over rough ground, 'that would be nothing compared to what our child will feel in the years to come when he or she understands that a family life would have been possible but for the pigheaded stubbornness of its mother…'

Mattie's mouth fell open at this unexplored avenue.

'You wouldn't,' she gasped.

'I would. Now, let's get going.'

Before she could leap off the bed he was moving swiftly towards the chest of drawers, where he began extracting her clothes, tossing them on the bed—in fact, on her.

The blankness in Mattie's head cleared and she scrambled up and began gathering the hurled items of clothing into her arms, while she demanded what he thought he was doing.

Dominic paused briefly to look at her. 'Getting you out of here, of course. You're coming back with me.'

'You put those things back! At once!'

'You'll wake the neighbours if you carry on shouting like that. Where do you keep your suitcase?' He didn't give her time to answer. Just checked under the sofa, which was the only place it was likely to be, and sure enough he extracted it, flipped open the lid and began stuffing her clothes in.

'The rest will have to wait until tomorrow. George and I will come and collect it all. How did you get here anyway? Who helped you move?'

'You can't do this! I'm not going to marry you, Dominic Drecos!'

'Tell me you didn't lug this stuff over in stages by yourself? In your condition?'

'In my condition?' Mattie was momentarily distracted by the old-fashioned nature of the observation. 'I'm pregnant, not ill!'

Dominic paused in what he was doing, which was surveying empty drawer number two with an expression of satisfaction. 'Well, you won't be doing any lugging around of anything when you're with me. You need to be taking things easy.' He stood up, flexed his muscles and then strode towards the small kitchen while Mattie scrambled off the bed in hot pursuit.

'I told you, I'm not—'

'Good. You kept a couple of boxes. That'll do for starters.' He picked up one of the cardboard boxes that she had stuck under the kitchen table when she had moved and promptly forgotten about. 'Sit down. I might as well get started here straight away. Less to pack tomorrow.'

Mattie sat down. Her legs felt shaky anyway. Well, they would do, wouldn't they, she thought a little frantically, considering she herself felt as though she had been suddenly stuffed into a tumble-drier that had been turned on full speed?

'You can't just waltz in here and take over my life like this!'

'I can and I am. Is this all the food you have in this

place?' He looked scathingly at the virtually bare kitchen cupboard. A jar of coffee, some sugar, some baked beans, pasta, a couple of cans of tuna. 'Have you been eating *at all*?' He slammed the contents of the cupboard into the box then turned to look at her narrowly and accusingly.

'Of course I have!' Guilt made her defensive and she glowered at him from under her lashes. This was all happening so fast. It seemed to her that after a life that had dragged on and on and on, everything had sped up the minute this man appeared on the scene. Their affair, her job, her hurt when she had discovered how he had manoeuvred her to get what he wanted, then the pregnancy. Now this.

'You barely touched your food tonight, I noticed.'

'Can you blame me? I was feeling just a tiny bit nervous about what I had to say to you!'

'Aside from anything else, you need supervision if you're not going to eat properly.' He opened the fridge, which was almost as bare as the cupboard.

'*Supervision?* Now you're being absurd. And will you please close that fridge? It has a habit of conking out if the door's held open for too long!'

Dominic shut the fridge very quietly, leant against it and gave her a long, hard look. 'Well, that says it all about this place. Your landlord ought to be reported. In fact, I've a good mind—'

'All right! I'll move back to the apartment. I'm sure Liz wouldn't mind…'

'You're coming with me and tomorrow we're going to go shopping. For a ring. Then we're going to arrange for a registrar. Then you're going to phone your parents and explain everything and I'll call mine.'

'I haven't even told Frankie,' Mattie whispered. She

might have missed the morning sickness but, thinking about it, she had been feeling very fragile recently. Prone to tears. That probably explained why she had spent every night crying since Dominic had disappeared from her life. No, of course it didn't.

But she was feeling very fragile now. Her head drooped and she rested it wearily on the table.

She was hardly aware of Dominic until she felt his hand stroke her downturned head. It felt strangely soothing. Then she heard him pull up a chair until he was sitting right next to her.

'What a mess,' Mattie said, twisting her head so that she was still draped on the table but looking at him now.

'Why do you find it so upsetting that you haven't told Frankie?' Keep it light, Dominic thought, unthreatening. But just the mention of that loser's name was enough to arouse a raw anger inside him. At a time like this, the last person he wanted her thinking about was her ex-boyfriend.

'It didn't even occur to me,' Mattie admitted.

Dominic felt the temptation to smile broadly. He adopted a serious, compassionate expression and continued to smooth her hair, her wonderful silky, fair hair that looked like spun gold between his long brown fingers.

'Why should it? Your mind's everywhere at the moment. I'm surprised you can think coherently at all.'

'I suppose.' She straightened up. Her eyes looked huge, like great big green pools, shimmering with unshed tears.

An unwelcome thought hit him like a physical blow to the head. What if, now that she had the virtue of comparison, she was beginning to think that what she had felt for Frankie had been love after all? That real love, the icing-on-the-cake kind of love, that she didn't feel for *him*? He knew he could be arrogant and yes, he supposed, selfish. What if she had begun to wonder whether her ex-boyfriend's laziness and who-gives-a-damn attitude might just be preferable to a monster who had made the mistake of trying to arrange her life to suit his purposes, which was how she thought of him?

Pain and uncertainty sliced through him like a knife and his jaw tightened. They added to the long list of alien feelings that had transgressed over those character traits which he had hitherto taken for granted, his iron self-possession, his talent for focus, his knowledge that he had his life utterly under his control.

'Well,' he stood up, impatient with himself, 'no point sticking around here. Let's go.' Dark, coolly determined eyes looked at her.

Mattie stood up as well but her mouth was stubbornly set in a line. 'I'll come with you, Dominic. But no rings and no arranging for a registrar.'

'We'll see.' He turned on his heel and headed for the door, *en route* collecting the suitcase he had earlier packed.

Discretion being the better part of valour, Mattie refrained from embarking on another fruitless argument with him. For the moment, she would go with him to his apartment and she would make sure to sleep in the spare bedroom. Tomorrow she would say what she had to say, make her compromises and clear out because she was desperately afraid that if she didn't she would end up doing just what he wanted her to do. Not because she believed that marrying him was the only option, but because the thought of just spending the rest of her life with the man she loved was so alluring.

It was all too easy for her mind to race ahead to a

scenario that had her trying to make him fall in love with her, enslaved by his natural charm, then watching as her efforts gradually began to repel him as she became as much of a nuisance as his last woman who had made the mistake of becoming obsessive.

Discovering the part he had played in getting her that job had brought her up short, and she knew that she had to cling to what she had learnt from the experience or risk going under.

Only when she was lying in her own bed an hour later did she begin to feel the strain.

She had got what she wanted, the spare room and solitude, but her victory seemed empty. And temporary. He had allowed her her little stand but for how long? He had pointedly not returned to any conversation about marriage, but she knew that in the morning he would resume his onslaught. And he hadn't touched her. Maybe he was saving that up as his trump card, knowing that she would melt in his arms just the way she always had.

The questions drove her crazy. She felt like someone poised to defend herself only to discover that the opponent was nowhere to be seen, especially when the remainder of the weekend was spent without further mention of rings or marriages or registrars.

They spent Saturday shopping. No jewellery stores but instead in clothes shops for her. She would need looser clothes, he assured her with a display of old-fashioned conventionality that would have been touching had she not been so busy protecting herself from getting drawn into the powerful net he was weaving around her.

He insisted on taking her to the food hall at Harrods, determined to find out whether she had any cravings, until she reluctantly ended up laughing at his suggestions. But still, he made sure to buy endless delicacies.

He was convinced that she had been foolishly starving herself because her supplies of food at the flat had been so pathetic.

And none of his concern was feigned. After the initial shock of her revelation, Dominic was surprised at how easy he found it to accommodate the thought of a child in his life. A child and a wife. Because she would be his, even though he knew that trying to force her hand as he had done to start with would serve no purpose whatsoever.

Had he forgotten just how spirited she was? She could be as stubborn as a mule and his mistake had been to think that she would docilely listen to his reasoning and do his bidding. Simply because he was so desperate for her to do so.

Surely he would be able to show her that life with him would not be the ordeal she anticipated? For someone whose life had been grounded in harsh reality, who had battled against all odds to achieve what she had achieved, she seemed to nurture sweetly romantic visions of love and marriage. And the vision didn't include him. Not yet.

He would have suggested going to see his country house the following day but they would have needed more than just a mere day there and there was no way he could spend longer, as he was going to be out of the country for the better part of the following week.

Mattie felt relieved and disappointed at this. Relieved that she would have some time to herself to decide just exactly how she was going to deal with the problem. Disappointed because, like it or not, she had lapped up his solicitous attention for two solid days.

He had been the epitome of the perfect father-to-be and to his credit he had not uttered a single word of recrimination about the sorry mess she had landed him in.

She wondered whether, by extension, she was supposed to see his performance as proof positive that he could be as agreeable a husband as he had been potential daddy.

If so he was mistaken, because every woman deserved love and love was the one word patently missing from their conversations.

'I trust I'll return on Thursday to find you here…' Dominic said with what she detected as warning in his voice as he was about to leave for work on the Monday morning.

'Well, I certainly won't be able to return to my flat, considering you collared the landlord, terrified the poor man by implying you would have inspectors on his back if he didn't do something about the state of the building and then told him that he'd seen the last of me.' Standing by the door, dressed for work herself, Mattie fought a tremendous urge to reach towards him and kiss those lips that had made a point of keeping away from her all weekend.

Maybe he was already tired of her, physically. Maybe the thought of her pregnancy had put him off her body. But no. He must have read her mind because he leant forward and placed his mouth on hers, a gentle kiss that was soon ignited into a burning, hungry flame.

Mattie found herself weakly clinging to the lapels of his jacket, pulling him towards her so that she could feel his probing tongue invade every inch of her.

She was shaking like a leaf when they finally drew apart. Trembling as though this were the first time they had touched. Whether she wanted to admit it or not, her body remembered his and wanted him back.

She turned away and Dominic was very tempted to pursue her before she had time to retreat, but he was playing a waiting game now, waiting for her to come to him.

Hell, how he wanted to touch her. Her breasts had become fuller now that she was pregnant and he could see them pushing against the grey wool jumper she was wearing.

Having her under his own roof for the past two nights, knowing that she was sleeping in a bed only metres away from where he was, had tested him almost to the point beyond endurance. Every time he had closed his eyes his head had filled with images of her and how she had squirmed sensuously in his arms, opened herself up for him, played her own games with his aching, responsive body.

Well, on Thursday he would be back and enough of all her procrastinations. He had been patient long enough and he knew that, for all her talk, she still wanted him as much as he wanted her. That single kiss had told him as much. Yes, she saw him as manipulative and her fierce independence reacted against that and yes, she had made it clear that, whatever she felt for him, love was not part of the equation, but she was carrying his child and he would marry her. By nature he was not a man capable of seeing his goal and then not doing something about attaining it. He had given her two days of space, during which time he had done his utmost to neutralise his responses to her on the premise that if she didn't fear him she would begin to see the logic of his arguments and would come to him willingly. Or as willingly as possible, given how she felt about him.

It hadn't worked. He could carry on pandering to her, allowing her to sleep in the guest room as if impervious to the glaring irony that, in the solitude of her single bed, she was pregnant by the man who was sleeping in the room next door. Caught between a rock and a hard place, Dominic wondered how long the charade would continue. Giving her ample time to get used to handling the situation with him there in a frankly supporting role.

And then would the day come when she just packed her bags and left so that she could continue what he had allowed but in the privacy of her own place? No. The answer was simple. Marriage, a shared bed, a life with him; all else could be sorted once those things were in place.

He left the apartment in a more contented frame of mind than he had felt for weeks.

Mattie, closing the door behind him, was far from contented. Every instinct in her rose up in fury at the way he smoothly, effortlessly and without much thought laid down his laws and expected complete obedience. So why did his obnoxious and ridiculous demand that they be married still dangle in front of her eyes with a niggling attraction?

She had said all the right things, laughed at his suggestion, pointed out how Victorian his thinking was, refused point blank to be coerced into a marriage that would be nothing short of a sham, but she couldn't carry on living with him here because if she did he would end up steamrollering over her objections. Love would make a fool of her yet again.

For the first time since she had joined the team, Mattie found that she was distracted at work. She volunteered to do some of the most intensely laborious work, just so that she could bury her head in ledgers and give her mind free rein to go where it wanted.

Was it too late to run away? she wondered. 'Course,

she couldn't; Dominic would find her and his rage would know no bounds. In any case, he was her baby's father and she could never run away from that moral obligation to her unborn child.

But she could leave his apartment. He was away until Thursday. Plenty time for her to pack her bags and go. Not to her own apartment, which was tinged with his handprint. Which only left one place. Frankie's.

At six-thirty, washed, changed and with the tiny black phone cupped in her hand, Mattie felt almost guilty as she made the call to Frankie. And as soon as she heard his voice down the end of the line, it hit her that the one thing she couldn't do was return to his house. That house, Frankie, all they had shared, now belonged to another world. She had taken giant strides since then, for better or for worse, and there was no going back.

But it was wonderful hearing his voice, especially in her fragile state of mind. On an impulse, she invited him over, deciding right there and then that she would tell him about her pregnancy when she saw him. Face to face. He wouldn't be able to tell her what she should do, but he wouldn't try and gloss over the uncomfortable reality either. One thing about Frankie was his simplicity when it came to dealing with situations. He had been unhappy and so he had taken to the booze, they had not been getting along and so he had avoided her. In the end, his solutions were far from commendable, but his bluntness now would cheer her up.

And she hadn't seen him for ages, could barely superimpose his face over Dominic's harsh, beautiful features.

When, forty minutes later, he arrived Mattie pulled open the door to someone whose image had faded from her mind so completely that it was almost like looking at a stranger. Frankie was shorter than she remembered and the good-looking face that had made her sixteen-year-old heart beat with girlish infatuation was almost bland compared to Dominic's aggressive good looks.

But then she blinked, smiled and a wave of affection rushed over her as she took in the indecisive way he was hovering and the small bunch of flowers languishing in one hand which he must have bought on the way over.

'You look bloody good, Mats.' He grinned and looked around Dominic's lavish apartment. 'All this high living suits you. Here, brought you these.' He thrust the flowers into her hands and gave the apartment another once-over with admiring eyes while she went to fetch him a lager.

'Off the booze, love.'

'You've *given up drinking*?'

Frankie looked sheepish as he followed her into the kitchen, dropping his bomber jacket on one of the chairs along the way. 'Had to. Couldn't get a job any other way, could I? After you did a runner and left me with all the bills to pay.'

Mattie swung around to find that he was grinning at her and she raised her eyebrows in a question.

'Yep. Got a job, would you credit it? Me! Old Bill down at the pub fixed me up with one of his suppliers and now I don't drink the stuff, Mats, I sell it.' He sat on one of the chrome and leather high stools at the counter. 'Somehow being surrounded by all that booze has kind of taken the glamour away. Now I just try and drink on weekends.'

'Off the booze. Got a job…mind me asking how come it never occurred to you to do that when I was around?' But she could see that his change in lifestyle suited him. He looked better. Had put on a little weight and there was a contentment about him that hadn't been there before.

And she was very happy that she had contacted him, felt guilty that she had not done so sooner. In fact, it hadn't occurred to her at all. Dominic had taken over her thoughts, her life and she had had nothing left over for anyone else.

The fact that Frankie's life seemed so sorted out made her feel even more hopelessly drained of all direction. She made them both some coffee, sat across the counter from him on another stool and found herself pouring her heart out.

Everything. No holds barred. She needed to tell *someone* and strangely enough, after all that time when their communication had drizzled away into arguments or stony silence, Frankie was actually listening to her, nodding, making all the right noises.

'So what am I going to do?' she asked, realising that she had managed to finish her cup of coffee and that she needed to stretch her legs. She stood up, scoured the fridge for some mineral water and then turned to look at Frankie questioningly.

'Marry the geezer. Don't see the problem myself, but then you always were as stubborn as a mule, Mats. You get something in your head and you can't find your way around it.'

'I should leave. I know I should, Frankie.' She poured some water into a glass and then swirled the glass around, peering in as though hopeful that the answers to her questions might be found somewhere there. Like a fortune-teller gazing at tea leaves and expecting to see the future in them.

'Why? And go where?'

Mattie shrugged and sighed.

'You can't go back to your rented place and anyway, be realistic, Mats, a man like that ain't going to let you live in squalor when you're having his baby. I mean, cock an eye at this lot!'

'That's just it, Frankie. He can't buy me and he doesn't love me so I need to get away.'

'No, you don't.' He sighed. 'Remember how we used to live, Mats? Running around like little vagrants? No treats, second-hand school clothes? Why choose that for a nipper when you can have the best?'

'Stop exaggerating. Besides, I'd have a job…'

'For how long?' He looked at her long and thought-fully, then dropped his eyes in a rare display of embarrassment. 'You can't afford anywhere really decent, not yet from what you've told me, and Mats, I'd love to help out, but there's a little problem there…'

'I wasn't asking you to.' But her curiosity had been piqued. 'Little problem…?'

'Your bloke's not the only one who's going to be a daddy.' Frankie's face was radiant and apologetic at the same time. 'Truth is, Mats, I was seeing someone before we broke up. Girl called Shannon. I hated myself for two-timing you and I know I took it out on you but I couldn't ask you to leave. I'm really sorry, Mats.' He sighed heavily and threaded his hair with his fingers. 'But she's moved in and somehow I don't think she'd like it if I was to offer a room to my ex.'

Surprise, belated hurt and pleasure for him because he was so obviously pleased with himself rushed through her. Pleasure won and she instinctively went to him and wrapped her arms around him, warmly aware of the affection they had once shared before time had eroded it.

And his arms folded gratefully around her at roughly the same time as a key was inserted into the front door and Dominic strode into the apartment.

CHAPTER TEN

'WHAT the hell is going on?'

Mattie and Frankie sprang apart like guilty lovers and underneath the dismay she felt a tide of joy that he was back. Even though his face was thunderously angry as he stormed towards them.

Frankie had jumped off the stool and was looking at Dominic with his hands in his pockets and his face wearing a bullish expression that Mattie recognised. He had never once raised his hands to her but he had been involved in enough bar-room brawls for her to know when he was tensing up for a fist fight.

The knowledge that he would lose to the powerful man glowering at him was enough to make her position herself very squarely between them.

'Nothing's going on, Dominic,' she said coolly. She had never seen him like this. Murderously angry.

'You're Frankie, are you? Well, if you want to stay in one piece then I suggest you clear out of my apartment before I throw you down all four flights of stairs.'

'Try it, mate.' But his voice sounded less confident than the words suggested. 'I was just going, as it happens.'

'Did you ask him over?' Dominic's brilliant black eyes focused on Mattie's white face and she nodded. He looked past her to where Frankie was still doing a good impression of a man who wasn't going to be pushed around even though his eyes were flitting anxiously to his discarded bomber jacket. 'Get out. Now. And don't even think of ever coming back here because you won't be invited a second time. Will he, Mattie?'

Mattie found herself just nodding, and by the time her senses had returned to normal Frankie had gone and Dominic was staring at her with blazing eyes from across the width of the sitting room. At which point she flared into anger.

'Did you have to act like a *thug*?' were the first words she could think of, which galvanised him into immediate action and had him standing inches away from her in the matter of a few seconds.

'He should be grateful I didn't break his neck!' Dominic grated, glaring savagely down at her. 'What the hell were you thinking, asking your ex-boyfriend over here? While the cat's away the mice will play? Couldn't wait to see the back of me so that you could pick the phone up and invite him around?'

Assailed by a tirade of accusations that made such little sense when added together, Mattie just remained silent and stared in bewilderment at Dominic, who threw her one last, scathing look before disappearing towards his bedroom.

Remaining where she was did not constitute an option. She found herself half tripping in his wake and reached the bedroom door as he was in the process of divesting himself of his shirt, which he proceeded to tear off his back and hurl onto the bed.

'I thought you were going to be away,' she said, mesmerised by the flexing of muscles in his shoulders as he moved. When he turned to face her, she hurriedly looked up and adopted her crispest *I-will-not-be-bossed-around-by-you* expression.

'Well, sorry to disappoint you, darling.'

'I know what you're thinking, Dominic...'

'I know what my eyes told me.' He unbuckled his belt and pulled it smoothly through the loops of his trousers, then it joined the discarded shirt.

'This is exactly why we can't get married!'

'And why would that be? Because you wouldn't be able to keep your hands off your ex-lover?'

'Because you're an arrogant swine!'

'I don't consider it arrogant to expect you not to invite old lovers into my apartment!'

'I...I needed someone to talk to.'

'You can talk to me!' Dominic bellowed. Every word leaving his mouth was wrong. He knew it and he couldn't help himself. She would never know what it had taken not to lunge at that loser and beat him to a pulp. Just seeing them with their arms around one another had been like a physical blow to the gut.

He was heading towards the bathroom. Now he stopped, turned around and said with savage grimness, 'Talk! You want to talk—well, talk!'

'Not when you're like this, in this mood.' Mattie turned her head away and he groaned softly as he saw the glimmer of tears. To walk away now would be the end of them. He knew it just as he knew that the end of them would be the end of him so he took a deep breath and walked towards her, expecting her to push him back, prepared to subdue her until she was willing just to let him hold her.

Instead, Mattie turned into him with a sigh of weary defeat and buried her head against his bare chest. She could hear his heart beating like a drum and when she put her palm flat against him she could feel it as well.

'I'm not in a mood.' He curled his fingers into her hair and pressed her against him. 'Correction. I am in a mood. I'm in a foul mood because I can't stand the thought of you having anything to do with that man. I can't stand the thought of you thinking of him, I can't stand the thought of you seeing him and I definitely can't stand the sight of finding you wrapped up in his arms.'

'Because you're jealous?'

Dominic gave a ragged laugh. 'Me? Jealous? Of someone like Frankie? Did you notice the way he started backing off when he thought I might go for him? Did you? He knew I could thrash him in seconds.' He smouldered for a while and then muttered savagely, 'But to answer your question, yes, I was.'

Mattie felt her heart melt as she acknowledged how much it would have taken for a man like Dominic to admit to that weakness. Except it didn't sound like weakness to her. In fact, it made her mind take flight and this time she couldn't bring it back down with prosaic internal lectures about common sense and cool, hard reason.

She wriggled free of him and stared up into his eyes. 'What are you trying to say, Dominic?'

'Nothing.' He turned away, his face darkly flushed.

'Oh, right. I had hoped…' Her head drooped and she walked towards the bed and sat down.

'Hoped? What…?' Dominic prompted, following her but, instead of sitting next to her, standing over her and seeming to hover. 'You were saying…?' he insisted, until Mattie raised her eyes to his.

'I don't love Frankie, in case you were afraid of that.'

Dominic half smiled foolishly, looked away, looked back at her. 'Of course you don't,' he swaggered in a way that made her want to smile.

'Which doesn't mean that I approve of your behaviour, although…I guess I understand. I shouldn't have asked him over. It was stupid of me.' She idly plucked at the duvet cover and sighed.

'He shouldn't have come.' She didn't love Frankie. He felt like a kid in a toy shop suddenly given a fistful of dollars. 'I suppose he was gutted when you told him about my baby?'

'The opposite, actually. Because he's going to be a father too.' Mattie lay down on the bed and stared up at the ceiling with her hands behind her head. 'He'd been having an affair for the last few months we were together.'

'The bastard,' Dominic growled, wondering how any sane man could have an affair when he was blessed with the fabulous woman stretched out in front of him. Then he issued a silent prayer to his rival that he hadn't felt that way about her after all.

Now he did sit on the bed. 'And did you mind?'

'Mind? That he'd been playing around behind my back? I wish he'd had the courage to tell me at the time, but no, I didn't mind. I was glad that he'd found someone, actually. Glad that he wasn't going to look at our relationship in retrospect through rose-tinted spectacles, because I know I don't.'

'Don't you?' He hesitated and then said, the words dragged out of him, 'Are you sure?'

Mattie propped herself up against the pillows, crossed her legs and looked at him with a slow smile.

She was tired of playing games. She might scare him but she would show her cards because she knew now that what he felt wasn't just lust. He really liked her. He would never have admitted to his jealousy if he hadn't. And from liking could easily grow love. Couldn't it?

'There's something I want to say to you.' Her voice shook slightly and she found that she just couldn't bear the way he was staring at her so intently. His body had stilled.

'What?' Dominic heard himself whisper.

'When we first met…well, when you first approached me…no…I'm not saying this the way I want to…'

'You don't have to say anything,' Dominic said roughly, scared that what she was going to say he would not want to hear. 'Just…just marry me. We can talk after.' Begging at this point. What kind of a man was he? He should have a demand in his voice, instead of this half-baked pleading he could hear.

'All right.'

The silence stretched between them like electricity, but before he could break it Mattie held up her hand to ward off what he had to say and breathed in deeply.

'Not because I don't think I have any choice. I do. Whatever you say, we could have a child and remain unmarried. No, I'll marry you, Dominic, because…' At this point her resolve began to falter.

'Because?' he prompted huskily.

'Because in any marriage, whatever you say, there has to be love, and I love you. Somewhere along the line, you broke down my barriers and I fell in love. I love you enough for the two of us and if that means that my heart gets broken, then so be it. I just can't fight any more.' She'd said it. Mattie closed her eyes on a sigh and lay back down with her legs still crossed.

She felt him edge towards her, but she was too afraid to open her eyes and look at him. 'I'll understand if you want to reconsider your marriage proposal, though,' she said unevenly.

'Could you…could you repeat what you just said?'

'You can change your mind about the marriage thing.'

'No, not that bit. The other bit.'

Now Mattie did open her eyes to sneak a look at him, to find him grinning at her like the cat that had got the cream.

'It's not funny,' she said dubiously, afraid to believe what her heart was telling her she should believe. Her heart, as she had learnt from experience, was not to be trusted.

'Yes. Yes, it is funny. It's very funny because...' He was still smiling like an idiot when he reached to touch her cheek with one finger. 'Because I came back here tonight to tell you the very same thing.'

Mattie wondered whether she had heard properly. 'You love me? As in...*love*? As in...*in love*...or just maybe *like a lot*?'

'As in the big thing. The big thing I've managed to successfully avoid all my life.' He lowered his head towards her and kissed her, a long, lingering kiss that seemed to last forever. 'I got to the airport and I thought, dammit, no way was I going to hop on a plane and disappear for four days. I kept thinking that I would get back to find that you'd disappeared, that I'd managed to frighten off the one woman in the world I wanted to spend the rest of my life with.'

'You did?' Mattie sank happily into the pillows. Now that he had started talking, she didn't want him to stop. She framed his beautiful face with her hands and drew him down to her. Practically fully dressed on a bed with him! A first. 'You thought that?'

Dominic raised one wry eyebrow and then shifted so that he was propped up and looking down at her. 'You don't want to hear the workings of my mind,' he murmured, giving her mouth little kisses.

'Oh, but I do! I've just spent so long thinking that the only thing you wanted from me was my body...'

'I admit that was the initial pull.' He shot her one of those slow, dangerous smiles that could make an iceberg melt. 'I'd been in a hellish relationship. When I saw you at the club, I was bowled over. In fact, I'd never had such a powerful feeling that I needed to make contact with a woman, wanted to have her. When you didn't respond the way I thought you would, instead of just shrugging and walking away I felt as if I was driven to pursue.'

'My poor Dominic. Feeling driven to pursue a woman must have been a shock.'

'You're enjoying this, aren't you?' Dominic teased. 'Do you like the thought of knowing that I'm utterly in your power?'

Mattie nodded lazily and smiled at him. 'It's a two-way thing,' she murmured.

'Oh, I know that.' She was just wearing a baggy cotton jumper and he continued looking at her as he divested her of the garment. 'No bra.' He cupped one of her breasts with his hands, then spread his fingers possessively over her stomach. 'I'm glad I didn't know that when I saw you wrapped up with your ex. I really would have sent him flying down those stairs.'

'And he wouldn't have deserved it.' Mattie coiled her arms around his neck and arched a little so that her nipples rubbed against his chest. 'I think he was a little floored by my emotional outpouring…'

'When you told him that you loved me?' Dominic asked with a trace of smugness in his voice that made her want to laugh. 'That he meant nothing to you? That I was the only man you had ever really loved…?'

'Something like that.'

'Good.' With one hand he began tugging down her

track-suit bottoms and she aided him by wriggling her legs free.

'And you're not upset about the baby?'

'Upset?' Dominic laughed with amusement at how inaccurate she was. 'I was overjoyed. You were pregnant and that gave me the perfect excuse for getting you to marry me. I figured that once we were married I would be able to make you see that it was the best thing you could ever have done.'

'I never suspected. I thought you were just taking responsibility and I was unwanted baggage that you felt duty bound to throw into the equation.'

'Little idiot.'

Mattie didn't quite know at what point they divested themselves of the rest of their clothes. She just knew that when they made love there was a sweetness and a feeling of utter happiness underneath the soaring passion.

And afterwards, with this new knowledge between them, they were able to pick up the thread of their conversation again.

'I never meant to manipulate you when I got you that job, you know,' Dominic murmured, one hand lying possessively on her breast, the other arm tucked beneath her head. 'I think I loved you then and yes, I admit I wanted you out of that house, away from that man, but I also fiercely believed that you could do the job. And then telling you what I'd done became more and more difficult, the more involved and dependent I got on you.'

'Dependent?' His words were music to her ears.

'Totally dependent. I went from being a man who couldn't stand the thought of a woman thinking she could influence me, to someone who was enraged because the one woman I had told I wanted with no strings attached took me at my word. I wanted you to be possessive with me because I was getting more and more possessive about you.'

'Good,' Mattie murmured with rapturous satisfaction. She slid her hand, very possessively, over his taut stomach and then down to where his proud manhood told her that she excited him as much as he excited her.

Dominic, repeating her action, felt her honeyed moistness on his fingers and he rubbed her just gently enough to make her squirm.

'I take it it's all right for us to be…doing this…? Making love won't harm the baby, will it…?'

'Oh, I think we're perfectly safe making love as often as we like.' Her breathing quickened in response to his sliding fingers and she moaned softly under her breath. 'Our beautiful baby will be born into a house filled with love. What could be better?'

Alexander Dominic Drecos was indeed born into love and he must have sensed it because he was the happiest of babies. Raven-haired and dark-eyed, he was the spitting image of his proud father and at eight months was crawling energetically around his nursery.

Their wedding had been a quiet affair, with none of the usual tentative ice-breaking necessary between the two sets of parents because Mattie's pregnancy was talking point enough, as was the excited long-range planning for the christening, which had taken place in Greece. Frankie and his girlfriend had come, with Dominic's blessing, as had Harry and a couple of the girls from the club Mattie had remained in contact with. And Dominic's country house, where they were now living, was large enough to more than accommodate Mattie's parents whenever they came up to visit. Which in turn provided them with the occasional opportunity to have a wicked weekend away in the London apartment.

Which, consequently, was where they were now, sprawled in the king-sized bed, replete after a languorous session of lovemaking that had begun at six, when they had returned from a hectic day's shopping, and had only been interrupted by the necessity to eat the Thai take-away that had been delivered to their door.

On these occasional weekends away, she had been amused to find that Dominic was more anxious about Alexander than she was. Now he was frowningly contemplating the possibility of an accident because his son's crawling had no respect for breakable objects, fragile items of furniture that had not been designed to be crashed into or doors that could unwittingly be opened unexpectedly against the head of an exploring infant.

Mattie allowed him his rant and then curled into him with a smile on her face.

'And here I was,' she murmured, tracing the outline of his mouth with a finger, 'thinking that I was woman enough to distract you from all your little worries…'

Dominic caught the finger and placed it between his lips so that he could suck it and watch her expressive face flush with pleasure.

'You know what you need, don't you?' she asked, before she could lose herself completely.

'Yes, I most certainly do, you adorable little witch…'

'Another child…' She allowed her inference to filter in and watched his face lovingly, that face that had once been so inscrutable and that now showed every loving nuance.

'You're not…'

'I am. I did the test this morning and I was saving it up to tell you.'

'Another *bambino*.'

'Or *bambina*.' Mattie laughed with delight at the expression on his face.

'Just like her *mama*.' He grinned and kissed the tip of her nose and not for the first time wondered what he had ever done to achieve such perfect happiness as this...

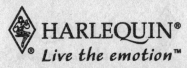

The world's bestselling romance series.

HARLEQUIN®
Presents

Seduction and Passion Guaranteed!

Mama Mia!

ITALIAN HUSBANDS

They're tall, dark…and ready to marry!

Don't delay, pick up the next story in this great new miniseries…pronto!

Pick up a Harlequin Presents® novel and you will enter a world of spine-tingling passion and provocative, tantalizing romance!
Available wherever Harlequin books are sold.

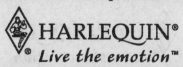

HARLEQUIN®
Live the emotion™

Visit us at www.eHarlequin.com   HPITHUSB

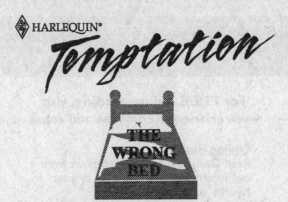

HARLEQUIN®
Temptation

THE WRONG BED

What happens when a girl finds herself in the *wrong* bed...with the *right* guy?

Find out in:

#866 NAUGHTY BY NATURE by Jule McBride
February 2002

#870 SOMETHING WILD by Toni Blake
March 2002

#874 CARRIED AWAY by Donna Kauffman
April 2002

#878 HER PERFECT STRANGER by Jill Shalvis
May 2002

#882 BARELY MISTAKEN by Jennifer LaBrecque
June 2002

#886 TWO TO TANGLE by Leslie Kelly
July 2002

Midnight mix-ups have never been so much fun!

HARLEQUIN®
Makes any time special ®

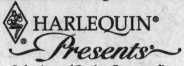

The world's bestselling romance series.

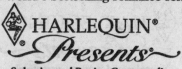

Seduction and Passion Guaranteed!

They're the men who have
everything—except a bride...

Wealth, power, charm—what else could
a heart-stoppingly handsome tycoon need?
In the GREEK TYCOONS miniseries you have
already been introduced to some gorgeous
Greek multimillionaires who are in need of wives.

THE GREEK TYCOON'S SECRET CHILD
by Cathy Williams
on sale now, #2376

THE GREEK'S VIRGIN BRIDE
by Julia James
on sale March, #2383

THE MISTRESS PURCHASE
by Penny Jordan
on sale April, #2386

Pick up a Harlequin Presents® novel and you will
enter a world of spine-tingling passion and
provocative, tantalizing romance!

Available wherever Harlequin books are sold.

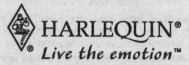

Visit us at www.eHarlequin.com